RANDOM

RANDOM

TOM LEVEEN

SIMON PULSE

New York   London   Toronto   Sydney   New Delhi

SIMON PULSE

An imprint of Simon & Schuster Children's Publishing Division

1230 Avenue of the Americas, New York, NY 10020

First Simon Pulse hardcover edition August 2014

Text copyright © 2014 by Tom Leveen

Jacket photograph copyright © 2014 by Yagi Studio/Getty Images

For information about special discounts for bulk purchases, please contact

Simon & Schuster Special Sales at 1-866-506-1949 or business@simonandschuster.com.

The Simon & Schuster Speakers Bureau can bring authors to your live event. For more

information or to book an event contact the Simon & Schuster Speakers Bureau at 1-866-248-3049

or visit our website at www.simonspeakers.com.

Book design by Regina Flath

The text of this book was set in Minion Pro.

Manufactured in the United States of America

2 4 6 8 10 9 7 5 3 1

Library of Congress Cataloging-in-Publication Data

Leveen, Tom.

Random / Tom Leveen. — First Simon Pulse hardcover edition.

p. cm.

Summary: The night before going on trial in a sensational felony case that has ruined her life,

sixteen-year-old Tori Hershberger receives a random phone call from

a stranger contemplating suicide and she begins a race against time to save him.

[1. Suicide—Fiction. 2. Conduct of life—Fiction. 3. Bullying—Fiction.

4. Family life—Fiction. 5. Popularity—Fiction. 6. High schools—Fiction. 7. Schools—Fiction.] I. Title.

PZ7.L57235Ran 2014

[Fic]—dc23

2013021006

ISBN 978-1-4424-9956-0

ISBN 978-1-4424-9958-4 (eBook)

RANDOM

ONE

They've been pounding on the front door for more than an hour, which is exactly how long it took for Dad to make his famous garlic mashed potatoes. He'd slammed the masher down time after time, *BAM! BAM! BAM!* with his lips drawn tight as Mom took measured steps between the stove and sink while making Italian meat loaf.

It feels like a last meal.

"I just want to ask a few questions, Victoria!" this one reporter keeps shouting through our closed door. Her name is Allison Summers. I've never met her face-to-face, still don't know what she looks like, but I know what she thinks of me, and what she made the rest of the world think of me. So she can stay out there and melt in the rain like the witch she is, for all I care.

None of us inside speaks. We just do our routine jobs,

but without saying a word. Normally Mom would be singing R.E.M. singles, or Dad would be reciting a stand-up routine from some dead comedian, or my brother, Jack, and I would be debating about whether or not Olympic athletes were "superhuman."

Tonight: a vast silence, like standing in an empty gymnasium.

Jack, in particular, makes it a point to not even look at me. I'm not used to this treatment from my older brother yet, even though he's been doing it for weeks. Mom and Dad are letting him do it too. That doesn't make me feel any better.

"Jack, where's the green napkins?" I ask as he pulls down plates.

He doesn't even point. I can see his jaw muscles working as he clenches his teeth, making his deep, pitted acne scars look like pulsing lunar craters. Jack had cystic acne all through high school, and people always called him all kinds of terrible names, even up till he graduated last year. Krakatoa, Pus Factory. Even Zit Face.

I never called him anything. He doesn't seem to remember that.

"Please, Miss Hershberger, this might be your only chance to set the story straight," Allison-the-reporter calls, pound-pound-pounding on the door some more.

"Check the other cabinet for the napkins, Tori," Mom says. She tries to make it casual, as if there aren't a bunch of reporters on our lawn in a light spring rain, but her voice is tight and strained.

So I check the other cabinet, and there are the green napkins, just where I knew they'd be. I'd asked only to see if maybe Jack would forget he wasn't talking to me and say something.

With Dad's potatoes done finally, we sit down around our small dining room table just off the kitchen. It's more of a nook than a room. We eat here six nights a week. Even now. Mom tries to smile at me as she gestures to the meat loaf, urging me to serve myself first.

"Victoria?" Allison Summers calls. "I'm on deadline. I'm filing a story tonight whether you talk to me or not, so you might want to think about telling people your side of things."

Another voice, male, shouts, "Have you decided on a plea?"

Dad's chair flips backward when he stands up. My stomach contracts and pulls me taut against my chair, and Mom drops a fork. Jack doesn't move, just sits there staring at his empty plate.

Dad races to the front door. I hear him fling it open.

"Get off my property!" Dad shouts. "Now! Every single last one of you, out!"

"Mr. Hershberger, I just want—"

"Out! I'll call the police on all of you, get out!"

"Mr. Hersh—"

"*Go!*" Dad roars, throwing a giant mother-F-bomb out with it. "You're nothing but a bunch of bloodsucking vultures! Get off my property and leave my family alone!"

I've never heard Dad swear before. Or yell. He's a grumbler, not a screamer.

"Thought we were supposed to ignore them," Jack whispers, not lifting his eyes.

"Easy for Mr. Halpern to say," Mom says, her voice wrenching a bit tighter. "He's probably having a quiet dinner."

I hear muttering at the front door, and a moment later it slams shut. Instead of coming back to the table, though, Dad stalks past us and goes down the hall and into he and Mom's bedroom. Another slammed door twists my stomach again.

At least the knocking has stopped. After a few more minutes I hear a couple of car engines start up and drive away from the front of our house.

I let out a breath I didn't know I'd been holding. Jack takes his napkin from his lap and tosses it on the empty plate.

"Are you even sorry?" he says.

I look up at him, blinking. These are the first words Jack's spoken to me in weeks. So of course I screw it right up.

"What kind of question is that?"

"A simple kind," Jack snaps. "Just answer it. Are you?"

"Jack," Mom says, "maybe now isn't—"

I'm too angry to let her even finish. I shout back at him, "Of course I am, Jack! God!"

Mom says, "Kids, please . . ."

Jack leans over the table, resting his forearms on the top. "Sorry you did it, or sorry you're in trouble?"

"What's the difference?"

Jack snorts and pushes his chair back. He stands up, takes one step, stops.

"God, Vic," he says. "I don't even recognize you anymore."

I try to come up with something to shoot back and come up empty. Plus, I kind of know what he means. I haven't *felt* much like myself.

"Jack," Mom says again.

"I've got homework," he says. "Might as well do some while I'm still enrolled."

"It'll work out, Jack," Mom insists. "Don't overreact."

Jack shrugs sarcastically. "Maybe overreacting is exactly what we should be doing," he says. He shoves his chair back under the table and goes down the hall to his room. He doesn't slam his door, but it doesn't latch quietly behind him either.

I look at Mom. She's rubbing her temples with two fingers each.

"Mom?"

Outside, a car passes by, going fast, it sounds like. Someone in the car performs a drive-by cussing, screaming out an open window before disappearing down the block.

"*Biiiiiiitch!*"

Mom's forehead, already creased, tightens.

"What, Tori."

"Um . . . nothing," I say, and get up. "I'm not very hungry."

Mom doesn't say anything. So I go to my room and close the door.

Maybe I should just plead guilty tomorrow. Maybe that'll make everyone happy.

Kevin Cooper wrote on your timeline.
August 26, two years ago.
Something tells me high school is going to suck, Hershy.

Tori Hershberger Maybe. But maybe not. Do NOT call me Hershy at school!!!

👍Kevin Cooper likes this.

Kevin Cooper Your a jock. Jocks always have more fun. :) And I won't call you that.

👍You like this.

Tori Hershberger Yeah, well, we'll see. ;) How's things with Rachel?

👍Kevin Cooper likes this.

Kevin Cooper Good.

Tori Hershberger Just good?

Kevin Cooper Just good. ;)

👍You like this.

TWO

"It's been six hours since dinner," I tell my friend Noah over the phone, "and I haven't eaten anything since lunch. I'm going to lose all my muscle if this keeps up."

Part of me wants a chicken burrito, and another part is like, *Yeah, right! Good luck keeping that down.*

"You gotta eat, Tori-chan," Noah says. "Jock need food, badly."

I don't answer. I know a bazillion girls who'd kill to have no appetite.

I feel myself wince. That was a poor turn of phrase right now.

"I wish I could sleep," I tell him. "Or do homework, even."

"You're definitely not feeling very good if homework is a reasonable alternative to sleep," Noah says. He's full of it. He gets straight As.

"Hard to do English without a computer," I say.

"True," Noah says. "But you could always use one of those, what do you call them . . . *pencils*?"

I'd probably laugh if tonight wasn't the night that it is. Still, Noah has a point. Maybe I could handwrite some things. Except I don't think my English teacher accepts anything less than twelve-point Times New Roman with one-inch margins. Mom promised to find a laptop from her work that would have an Office suite on it or something, but so far she hasn't. We've all been a *little* preoccupied. But if I don't start turning some things in, there goes junior year.

Speaking of next year . . .

I'm sixteen now, which means if things go badly, I won't get out of prison till I'm twenty-six.

I don't say that to Noah as I sit at my empty desk, holding my phone to my ear and listening to him eat something. Probably popcorn. It's not crunchy enough for chips. I'd hear it if it was chips.

I hate my new phone.

Wait; I should be careful using a word like *hate* right now too. In fact, I'd be happy to never hear it used again.

I should also use quotes around the term "new" phone. It's not *new*-new. Mom had been meaning to recycle it for more than a few years now. It's been sitting on the kitchen counter, in a little clay dish I made in first grade, along with a stew of paper clips, rubber bands, and an outdated Burger King coupon nobody's bothered to throw away. The coupon is so old, it's a family joke. "Hey, buy one, get one free at Burger King!" we'll say whenever someone asks Dad what's for dinner. Mom always sighs and says she knew Canyon City was getting too big when we had *two* Burger Kings instead of one.

Well, at least I've *got* a phone. They didn't completely take away my ability to communicate with the few people who still care to acknowledge me. Which, can I just say, is so hypocritical. As if my teammates didn't give Kevin Cooper a hard time at school. As if the entire coaching staff didn't have it in for him during PE. My God, if ever there was a person who gave Cooper a bunch of crap, it was Coach Scordo, who runs the baseball team and all the boys' PE classes. Any guy who couldn't run a lap got ostracized; I'd seen it. And did administration or the rest of the staff do anything about it? No. Why aren't *they* in trouble too?

Whatever.

I sigh out loud and trace a finger on top of my desk. In addition to switching my phone, my parents also confiscated my laptop, and thus, my lifeline to the wider world. There's still a rectangular dust pattern on my desk from where it used to sit. I should clean that up.

Maybe tomorrow.

"So, Tori-chan?" Noah says on my new/old phone. "You're being awfully quiet. Dare I ask what's on your mind this fine evening?"

"Don't you watch the news?" I ask back. "You know what tomorrow is."

I almost tell him to stop calling me "Tori-chan" instead of just Tori, but right now anything other than Victoria Renée Hershberger is a relief. The TV reporters insist on using all three names, like they do with assassins: Lee Harvey Oswald, John Wilkes Booth. . . .

Hershberger. There is one word to describe this surname: *ghastly*. It looks god-awful beneath last year's freshman Canyon High yearbook photo the news uses all the time. It crowds across my shoulders on my jersey. And it definitely didn't sound any better coming from that stupid reporter during dinner.

"Of course I've been watching," Noah says. "But I don't expect them to tell me the truth."

"I love you," I say.

Noah laughs. "Don't let your mouth write checks your heart can't cash, Hershy."

He's the only person left on planet Earth I'd ever let get away with calling me something like "Hershy." But we go back a long time. Sixth grade. That's virtually an eon. We hung out a lot more back then, in junior high. Even last year. We sort of drifted this year, though. Which makes me all the more grateful that he's sticking by me now.

I lie flat on my bed, staring at the ceiling. "Hey, can you eat a popcorn ceiling?"

"The question is, why would you want to?"

"Because it's popcorn. Duh."

"Pretty sure it's not real popcorn, Tori-chan."

He loves to hear himself say that. Noah wants more than anything to live in Japan. He has this whole spiel about the difference between *-chan* and *-san*. It's cute, but also stale. He's been in love with all things Japanese ever since he first saw *Fullmetal Alchemist*. The obsession grew from there.

"More important, would it taste good with butter and salt?" I say, and answer my own question. "Yes. Everything tastes better with butter and salt. I'd eat my own feet with butter and salt."

"Your own feet, huh?"

"I mean, I'd wash 'em first, obviously."

"That's good, 'cause I've smelled your cleats after a game, and *man*. . . ."

"Shut up."

"Seriously, you guys need to clean up better."

"Says the man crushing on our entire infield."

"Just the infield?" Noah says, feigning shock. "It's the whole team, Hershy."

"I was trying to keep you from sounding like a man whore."

"Yeah, well, man whores get dates," Noah says. "So when's your next game—"

He cuts himself off. I won't be at a game for quite some time. Like, next year, maybe. If I'm lucky. Apparently he forgot.

Or is it *allegedly* he forgot? I can't keep track anymore.

"Well," Noah says after a pause, "I guess, whenever you come back, huh?"

"Yeah," I say. "Sure."

I hear him sigh. "So why'd you call me? To talk about eating your ceiling?"

"Maybe."

"Look, Tori, if you're so totally opposed to talking about it . . ."

"Sorry," I say, very bitchy—bitchily? "Forget it."

I hang up, closing the flip phone. A *flip phone*. A cheap and outdated substitute for my iPhone. May as well be chiseled out of granite. I dump the flip onto my nightstand and fling an arm over my eyes to block out my overhead light. Feels like an interrogation room in here with that blazing corkscrew bulb. "Soft white light," my muscular *ass*.

I didn't mean to be bitchy to Noah, but God, I need a distraction, not more talk about the case. I've been living and breathing nothing else for like a month now. Can't we just talk about dumb things like . . . like popcorn ceilings? Or how hot he thinks Alexis and Alyssa and Taylor and Megan and the rest of the team are?

I wish they'd call me.

Anyway. For all the terrible things about to happen to me, it's kind of a relief to be cranky about my phone or that the light is too bright in here or that my name is so dumb. It's comforting. Reality. Such normal things to be pissy about.

The phone rings, vibrating on the nightstand. *Reeee. Reeee. Reeee.*

I look at my clock. The red digital letters blink from 11:53 to 11:54. A single red dot illuminates the p.m. window. It looks so lonely out there on its own, that little red dot. Doing the same old job, day in, day out. *The time is currently post meridiem,* the little red dot says. *Just so you know.*

Am I getting weirder? Is this what happens when you can't leave the house? Maybe it's cabin fever or Stockholm syndrome or something. Wait, no, that's kidnappers. Whatever.

I pick up the phone and check the teeny-tiny LCD screen. It's Noah on the ID. He's one of the few people whose number I have, and that's only because he called me. If he hadn't, I'd have lost his number forever. It's not like I had it memorized. I didn't have *anyone's* number memorized. Mom and Dad didn't even take me to the Apple store to try to download my contacts onto the flip before they took my iPhone. They just took it and came back later with this piece of crap.

A contact number transfer probably wouldn't have worked anyway; the technology is too dated on the flip phone. It would've been like teaching Neanderthals to drive a sporty coupe.

"You shouldn't hang up on people like that," Noah says after I open my phone back up.

"Why not?"

"It's rude," he says.

"I've been called worse," I say.

"Don't start that," Noah says.

"Sorry," I say, not bitchily this time. "Can't much help it."

The next words that almost come out of my mouth are, *Noah, I am so scared.* But I don't let them. It won't help.

"So what's your plan tomorrow?" Noah asks, trying very hard to make it a casual question when it is anything but.

My stomach clenches from the inside out, like a series of fists doing a hand-over-hand on my softball bat.

"Try not to pass out, I guess," I say.

"Man, I'm sorry, Tor," Noah says, sympathizing instead of pushing me to divulge my plan for court like those reporters tonight. Like the rest of the world. They can wait a few more hours, all of them.

Noah's willingness to let me not talk specifics is one of the reasons I'm friends with him. He doesn't go straight for the gossip, straight for the big scoop, like the girls on the team would have. Maybe it's better they haven't called, after all.

"I know it's probably a long shot, but is there anything I can do?" Noah asks.

His voice is calm and gentle. I've never kissed Noah, but I would totally make out with his voice if that were possible. His voice and Lucas Mulcahy's arms. Perfect.

I yawn. Finally. I would've gone to bed an hour or two ago except I can't get my mind to stop trampolining. Or, is that a word? Did I just make up a new word? Cool.

"I don't think so," I say to Noah.

"You sure?"

"Yeah," I say. "It's late. I should go to bed."

"Early day at school?" Noah says.

It's a bad joke. Very bad. I don't even have to point it out.

"Sorry," he says right away. "That was stupid. Didn't mean it."

"It's okay," I tell him. "I know. I get it."

"Everyone misses you."

"No, not everyone."

"*I* miss you."

"Thanks," I say, but I'm thinking of Lucas when I say it. Does *he* miss me? The one guy I really want to miss me, I'm not supposed to talk to anymore. I wonder what Lucas is doing tonight? Are those big hands wrapped around a pillow, or folded carelessly beneath his head as he sleeps, confident in his plea tomorrow? What about Marly and the others? Are they already asleep too? I wonder if Lucas is worried. I doubt it. I wonder if he's worried about *me*. I doubt it.

Then I wonder how expensive *his* lawyer is. I'll bet he charges more than Mr. Halpern.

Now I've bummed myself out. Again.

"Noah?"

"Yo."

"What do *you* think I should plead?"

I hear Noah blow out a breath, and imagine him rubbing his eyes with one hand as he says, "Jesus, Tori."

"I'm serious," I say. "I mean, you knew him too. Why don't *you* hate my guts?"

It's so quiet for so long, I imagine I can count each individual drop of rain on my awnings.

"Noah?"

"Look," he says suddenly, "you're right, you should get some sleep. It's probably gonna be a tough day tomorrow, yeah? So just . . . you know, turn off your phone, kill the lights, listen to some music or something . . . just give yourself a break."

"Why aren't you answering the question?"

"I don't—I don't *know* what you should plead, Tori," Noah says. "I know that I don't hate your guts, that I could *never* hate your guts, that I've always—"

He stops. I listen.

"Just shut everything off and forget about it," he says finally. "Okay?"

Not the response I was hoping for. But then again, I'm not entirely sure *what* response I was hoping for.

"Okay," I say. "I'll call you tomorrow when it's over."

Except it won't be over, I think. *It will have just gotten started.*

"Well . . . I dunno, I could stay up or something," Noah says abruptly. "I'm pretty amped on caffeine right now, I can talk if you want. I'll be up anyway. I'm gonna do a chat with some guys in Tokyo. Which probably also means I'll be ditching tomorrow."

"Thanks, but I'm sure," I say. "I'm going to go to sleep. At least, I hope so."

Another pause. He seems to be taking his time answering now. I wonder if I've totally scared him or just made him uncomfortable.

"Okay," Noah says. "Later on. And hey, Tor?"

"Yeah."

"You'll be okay."

Hisssss. A drop of acid burns my eye. At least, that's what it feels like.

"Thanks," I say as salt water pools at the back of my throat.

I end the call before he can say anything else, and toss the phone back to my nightstand.

Thank God for Noah. Despite hearing what the media says about me, he's still around. I'll bet everyone at school only watches the news because they want to see if their particular interview was used or not. Will their *genuine insights into the tragedy* make national news, or just local?

It's probably easy to wish for fame when the spotlight's not on you. Fame sucks.

The flip phone buzzes. I look at the screen, expecting it to be Noah. Who else would it be? Who else *could* it be? I didn't even have Lucas's or Marly's numbers before *or* after my iPhone got taken away. Which honestly makes me mad. Lucas would always give me this look at lunch, like a secret look, you know? Or throw an arm over my shoulders in the hallway sometimes. I thought he was starting to feel the same way about me as I did about him. So what if he put his arm around Marly sometimes too? And Dakota. And some of the cheerleaders.

Whatever. We're not supposed to communicate, anyway. Something tells me *they* are finding a way to do it, though— Lucas and Marly and Dakota and Steve and the other guys. It's just a gut feeling. Maybe because they've known each other longer, or because they're juniors . . . I don't know.

Still staring at the phone screen, I wonder if maybe it's one of my girls, my teammates, finally making contact, ending the big freeze. If I'm found not guilty, will they let me back on the team? Is that what it'll take? Maybe I should ask Coach Hayes. Except she hasn't called either. You wouldn't think a JV softball team in a two–Burger King town could have PR problems of a kind that would make teammates and coaches bounce away like scrimmage balls from a spilled bucket. But I guess it can.

I don't recognize the number at all. It's a local area code but not the same as mine. I shouldn't answer it. It's a crank call. Or worse. "Crank" doesn't really do the term justice. Since I haven't been online in a month, I can only assume someone tracked down my cell number and posted it on Facebook or something, so that everyone on earth can call me and talk trash.

I'm used to it.

I think.

I can't believe my parents went to all the trouble to activate this crappy phone but didn't bother to change the number. Awesome. I need to ask them to correct this.

I flip the phone open, fully expecting a barrage of cusswords. I spent most of last night writing down a list of fantastic compound, hyphenated swearwords and insults to fire back at the crank callers. I could diagram swearword sentences, sort of like back in eighth grade, when everything was okay and you knew who your friends were.

The red digital numbers blink from 11:59 to 12:00. The single red dot disappears from the p.m. window.

I say, not really caring:

"Hello?"

And no one responds. But I hear something like static. No,

not static. Rain. It's still raining here, too. Harder than during dinner. The patter of it taps on the aluminum awning over my window so fast, it's become monotonous white noise. I think it's similar to what I hear on the other end of the phone—rain tapping and plopping and fading into static.

"If you're going to call me names or something, go ahead," I say to the caller. "Because I've already put your number into Google, and I am more than happy to pay the twenty bucks or so it'll cost me to find out who you are and where you live."

I'm bluffing, of course, as I have neither Google nor money. I probably won't even end up with any of the money Dad put away for school, due to paying Mr. Halpern.

God*dammit* I'm in so much trouble.

"So?" I say. "Go ahead. Just a few more clicks and I'll know everything about you, so you may as well enjoy calling me a bitch or whatever."

Another sound from the other end. A sniffle, I think. A single, stealthy snort. Which is a great name for a children's book. I don't think I'll ever be allowed to write one of those, either. Do publishers do background checks? What about professional softball teams? Will all of this have to go on my college apps?

The caller says, "Why would I call you a bitch?"

It's a guy.

His voice is a flatline, monotone, like the rain. Bit of a rasp to it, like he gargled with 10 percent sandpaper solution, or sings in a hard-core band and had a gig last night.

"I, um . . . I don't. . . . Who is this?"

"Andrew," he says. "Who is *this*?"

"You mean you don't know?" I say.

"No."

"Then why'd you call me?"

Another sniffle. Maybe Andrew has a cold. That's what you get for sitting in the rain.

"It was at random," Andrew says. "I didn't think anyone would actually answer."

He grunts, or maybe laughs, but not in a "Something struck me funny" way. It sort of comes out his nose in a *humph* sound.

"Seriously?" I say, because I can't for one second believe this isn't another crank call.

"The complete randomness of it was the whole point," Andrew says.

I should just hang up, and I know it. But now I'm intrigued. Especially if he really isn't pranking me. Plus, the prankers don't usually take this long. They just call me some name and hang up. Like the car that drove by tonight: *Biiiiiitch!*

Can I just say how unique and clever that one was? It's better than another brick through one of our car windows, though. I guess.

"Ohhh-kay," I say, "why are you calling people at random at midnight on a Thursday, Andrew? Because honestly I was about ready to go to bed."

I don't bother to say, *And stare at my popcorn ceiling for a few hours before getting back up and pacing and lying back down and getting back up and so on,* which is really closer to the truth. Hungry and exhausted, unable to eat or sleep. Woo-hoo.

I *really* need to get some rest for tomorrow. Noah was right. I should've turned the phone off completely.

"Why'd I call you?" he repeats back to me. "Well, that's kind of a long story. Sorry, I'm just . . . still surprised anyone picked up. Wow."

"Right, you expressed your dismay already."

"Not dismay. Shock. Like . . . I dunno, like maybe God's really there after all."

I sit up and dig the fingers of my left hand into my scalp. And yawn.

"Yeah, well, don't get your hopes up," I say. "Now why are you calling me again?"

"Can I ask you something?"

I give him a dramatic sigh. "I guess."

"Do you think God really exists?"

"No," I say. The certainty of it in my voice startles even me.

"How come?"

I take more time answering now. "Because life's not fair."

"Yeah," Andrew says slowly. "I hear ya."

No, you don't, I think. *You have no clue just how bad it can get.* Instead of pointing this out, though, I say, "Now can I ask *you* something?"

"Um. Sure. Why not."

"Why'd you call this number allegedly at random?" There's that word again. *Allegedly.* Maybe if I repeat it enough times, it'll lose its meaning.

I hear the mystery caller take and release a deep breath.

"Honestly?" he says.

"Yeah, honestly."

"Well, honestly . . . because I'm going to kill myself."

Reeee. Reeee. Reeee.

The sound is not my phone buzzing. This time the buzz is in my ears, in my head, a bazillion wasps stinging gray matter.

"You *fucking* dick!" I scream, and slap the phone shut.

So much for my sweet list of compound swearwords. Had to fall back on a classic.

Doesn't make it less true.

Dick. I should've known.

Conversation started October 16, two years ago.

Kevin Cooper did you get our history assignment?

Tori Hershberger Yeah. Where were you today?

Kevin Cooper had to go home

Tori Hershberger Sick?

Kevin Cooper Not exactly. I'm surprised you didn't hear. didnt Jack tell you?

Tori Hershberger Seniors don't talk to FRESHMEN remember? :) Tell me what?

Kevin Cooper big black Magic Marker. my forehead. one word: "pussy."

Tori Hershberger Are you kidding? Who did it?

Kevin Cooper I dont know them. baseball players.

Tori Hershberger Do I know them?

Kevin Cooper doubt it. sophmores or jrs I think.

Tori Hershberger Sorry, Cooper. :(

THREE

Mom simultaneously opens my door/sticks her head in/ knocks. It is not one of her more endearing traits. What if I'm shooting heroin in here? Or solving string theory equations? Or *rubbing one out*, as Jack likes to say. And do. More times than I can count, I laughed my head off as Mom did her open/peek/knock routine at Jack's door and Jack screamed "Mooooooooom!" at the top of his lungs because he was getting handy with his unit. *Cracked* me up.

I wish he'd start talking to me again.

"Tori?" Mom says, and puts one bare foot past the threshold. Her eyes are squinty, like she just woke up, but she's still in her bathrobe.

"Tori's not available right now," I say, covering my eyes again.

I hear her slide over my wine-red carpet to the bed, and feel the mattress bend beneath her slim weight as she sits near my knees. I'm built more like Dad. Good thing I like sports, I guess.

"I heard you, uh . . . shouting. . . ."

"Sorry," I say. But I'm not.

"Another phone call?"

"Yeah."

She sighs. "Maybe you should just give me your phone."

"No! Mom, come on. . . ."

"All right, all right," she says.

"How about you have my number changed?"

"We didn't think about it, honey," Mom says. "Why not just turn it off and go to bed, hmm?"

Instead of answering that clearly ridiculous suggestion, I say, "When can I have my computer back? How bad could it be?"

"Well . . ." Mom tries to secretly roll her eyes, but fails. I see it clearly, and just as clearly it reads as, *It could be really, really bad, as a matter of fact.*

They didn't have to tell me why they took my laptop and switched my phone. I knew. They didn't want me to see what people were saying about me. About *all* of us. I thought I could handle it fine, until I spent one entire night scrolling through comments on our local newspaper website. Ten full screens of comments about us, not just from Canyon but from all over the country.

It's not an easy thing, knowing there are people out there who would happily kill you.

Never mind the irony of it, of wanting to murder someone

accused of what I'd *allegedly* done. When Mom found me at six in the morning, shivering on my floor, unable to stop seeing the parade of awful and sometimes violent words being spewed at me and the others, that was it for me on the Web.

Remembering all that makes me ask, sort of to myself and sort of to Mom, "Why can't they just leave me alone?"

Even *I* know how whiny that sounds. But it's a fair question. Don't they have other people to bother? Oh yes! Six of them. Instead they call me. I don't know, maybe they call Lucas and Marly and the others, too, and I just don't know it since we can't talk anymore.

Mom doesn't answer my question. And I know why. It's because every possible response will make me look terrible.

Sometimes people just make bad choices. Like me.

They're not thinking clearly. I certainly hadn't.

They're just rude, and obnoxious, and they're projecting their worries onto someone else. Me too.

I could go on. They all could be said about me, and that's why she's not answering.

"You should get some sleep," Mom says finally. "Tomorrow's a long day."

"Oh, gee, *is* it?"

"Tori . . ."

"Sorry," I say again. But I'm not. Again.

Would it matter if I was? I mean, what does *sorry* have to do with anything anymore? Maybe I should ask Jack if it really matters.

"Good night, honey," Mom says.

Until recently, she would've kissed my forehead and both cheeks and nose, in that order. Nobody else knows she does that; it's just between us. It's a holdover from when I was little. I guess I'm not little anymore.

I peek from beneath my forearm and watch her go out, turning for her bedroom. Dad's already asleep. I can tell because he's not laughing at whatever's on Comedy Central.

But then I haven't heard him laugh in a while anyway, so maybe he is up and I just don't know it. I haven't seen him since dinner.

Mom didn't shut my door, another one of her fine habits, so I get up and close it myself.

Reeee. Reeee. Reeee.

My phone vibrates on the nightstand. Are you kidding me?

I look at the LCD. It's the same number as before. *Andrew.* If that's even his name.

"Don't," I tell myself. "Just don't even bother."

I grab one of my softballs off the floor and juggle it between my hands. I really miss going to practice and the games. A lot. Until this whole mess, I'd been playing better than the varsity girls, and Coach Hayes knows it. Now it looks like the season is over for me after only two games, so I don't know what that means for varsity next year. I don't know if I'll even be *at* that school next year.

I don't know if I'll even be *in* a school next year. . . .

Reeee.

"Random number, my ass," I say to Andrew while tossing the ball behind my back and catching it.

Reeee.

"If you think I'm going to just—"

Reeee.

"—buy into that crap . . ."

Reeee.

My eye falls on my backpack, gathering dust on the floor by the foot of my bed. I can't help but notice the tiny smi ley face Kevin Cooper drew on it early last year. The face is rendered in silver ink, smiling up from one shoulder strap. We were so tiny then. Fifteen, and barely. I was headed into algebra and Kevin was headed into geometry, and I guess he must've remembered how much I had hated our math teacher back in junior high, how she used to give me stomach cramps. And he just whipped out this silver Sharpie and drew the smiley on my backpack and said, "No worries."

I got a B that semester.

Reeee.

What if Andrew is for real? I mean, I know he's *not*, but just what if?

Reeee.

No. You know what? It's not real; how could it possibly be real? The guy's a jerk like all the others, and if he wants to go a few rounds of Cuss Out, fine. Let's go. Not like I'll be sleeping anytime soon, anyway.

I toss the softball onto my mattress, grab my phone just a

split second before it would've gone to voice mail, and flip it open.

"What?" I bark.

This is such a bad idea. But then what's the worst he can do? Call me a bitch? Ooo. That'll leave a mark.

Except it kind of does.

I start scanning my mental list of profanities, which is probably why I get so derailed by what he says first.

"You're still there," Andrew says.

"Yeah, so?" I say. "Get it over with."

"Get *what* over with? What are you talking about?"

I throw another sigh at him, and roll my eyes even though he can't see me. "Like you don't know," I say.

"I'm sorry," Andrew says. "I guess I probably shouldn't have just jumped right into that."

"Oh, gee, jumped right into what?"

"You know," Andrew says. "The whole suici—"

"Do you know who this is?" I say. "Do you have any idea who I am?"

"Well, no, like I said, I—"

"You called this number at random," I interrupt. "You really expect me to believe that? That is one weak-ass, made-up story."

He doesn't say anything.

But he doesn't start swearing at me either.

"You're right," Andrew says, and clears his throat. "I shouldn't have bothered. Stupid idea. Sorry to bug you."

Silence. He already hung up.

"Good," I say.

Except I don't feel good.

Something about what he said, or maybe it was how he said it—

No. There's no way. Nobody decides to . . . do what he said he was going to do but makes one random phone call beforehand.

I mean, I doubt it.

I don't think.

Do they?

I'm sorry.

Do you think God really exists?

Stupid idea.

Not at all similar to the things people who've cranked me have said. Jackie Thompson called and said she hopes I get the death penalty. Some other kid called to inform me I was destined for hell. Other people whom I never identified for sure called to drop C- and F-bombs on me.

The worst part really is the girls, the other Canyon High JV softball Spartans, my good-old teammates, who have not been cranking me, not been calling me names, and not saying *anything*. Not even stopping by the house to check in. Probably getting all their news from—well, the news. And Facebook.

Stupid *f'ing* Facebook . . .

Anyway. This Andrew guy, it's some kind of elaborate joke. It's got to be. Big setup, big punch line. Joke's on me, ha-ha. It's probably those Christian Young Life kids. Irony not included. People think *I'm* a bitch? How about that whole "let she who has no sin throw the first stone" bit?

I hear the squeaky cabinet door complain in the kitchen. I think every kitchen on earth has that one cabinet door. No matter how fast or slow you try to open it, it always screeches. And you can coat the thing in a spray of WD-40, top to bottom, front to back, and never find the source of that squeak.

It must be Jack. I'm sure Mom and Dad are in bed by now, and we keep the coffee in that cabinet.

I get up and go into the kitchen. Jack's dumping coffee grounds into the machine and going to great lengths not to see me standing there.

"So this douchebag guy just called," I say, noticing that Mom didn't bother to save Dad's mashed p'tats. Well, they looked lumpy anyway. Uncommon for Dad. *That's* probably my fault too, I'm sure.

Jack doesn't answer. He flips the lid down and taps the on button.

"Some jerk," I go on. I force a dismissive laugh, but it sounds like a vomit hiccup. "Said he was going to kill himself."

All I need is for Jack to half grin, or shake his head, or thump me on the shoulder. Something. Anything to indicate a tiny little bit of empathy or even sympathy.

"Oh yeah?" Jack says to my surprise. He crumples up the coffee bag and jams it into the trash. "What'd he want, advice on how to do it?"

Nice. How's that for a fastball to the tits?

"No," I say, folding my arms and feeling like a child. "It was just another stupid crank."

Jack snorts. "Guess you better hope so, huh?"

Something electric and black races up my spine. "What's that supposed to mean?"

"Geez, Tori," he says, making a great show of squinting at the coffeepot, where the water hasn't even started to percolate yet. "Someone says they're gonna kill themselves, and you hang up on them. Guess that's about par for the course, huh? We *do* need to use a sports metaphor here so you can understand it, right?"

Jack walks past me, taking care not to let our clothes, much less our skin, touch. I pivot on my heel to follow him with my eyes.

"I didn't hang up on him!" I say, which, while entirely true, isn't the whole story either.

Jack doesn't so much as grunt. Just keeps going.

"Are you ever going to talk to me like a normal person again?" I say as he heads for his room.

"Go to hell, Victoria," he says, without stopping or turning. "Or offsides, or the penalty box, or wherever it is you people go."

Then he's in his room and the door's shut.

"I'll take that as a no," I say, but not loud enough for anyone to hear. I go into the kitchen, unplug the coffeemaker. Ha. That'll show him. Show him what, I don't know exactly, but it feels good to stick him a bit.

I go back to my room and close the door. Then, absurdly, I check my phone for a message. Nothing.

So that proves it, right? That proves that "Andrew" was just some jackass whose voice I didn't recognize. Not, like, a real person.

A real person really considering—you know.

But then . . .

What if Jack's right?

What if I wake up tomorrow and find out some guy really did hurt himself? I should call Mr. Halpern. Tell him what's happened. No, it's midnight. *After* midnight. Okay, I'll call . . .

I'll just call—

Is there anyone *left* to call?

Yes. I grab the phone and scroll through my recent calls to Andrew's number.

He'll pick up and start laughing, I tell myself. *When he does that, I can cuss him out and just go to sleep.*

He'll pick up and call me a bitch, and then I'll hang up and go to sleep.

After the third ring I hear myself chanting, "Pick up. Pick up. Pick up."

Because if he doesn't answer—

If he doesn't answer, that just means he went to bed. Or something.

Right?

Pick up, pick up.

But he doesn't.

Friend Requests

Marly DeSoto [Confirm] [Not Now]

FOUR

The line stops ringing. I hear the same static-like rain in the background, but no one says anything.

"Hello?" I say.

"Yeah," Andrew says. Not kindly.

Something uncorks in my belly and empties out through my feet. Relief, maybe?

"I thought—I mean, for a second, I was afraid that . . ."

"That what."

I chew around for some words. "You're not serious, are you?"

He gives that same snort-laugh thing that he did earlier. "Does it matter? Does *anything*?"

"Look . . . Andrew, right?"

"Yeah. Thanks for remembering."

I ignore the sarcasm. He's not very good at it.

"Andrew, listen, if you're even remotely the tiniest bit serious about . . . what you're talking about doing, and I sort of doubt you are, you have to know I am absolutely *the* most—I mean *titanically* wrong person on the planet you could be speaking to right now."

He sniffs.

"Why's that."

"Victoria Hershberger?" I say. "You haven't heard that name recently?"

"Should I have?"

Maybe I'm not as famous—or notorious—as I'd feared. Wouldn't that be nice.

"How old are you?" I ask.

"Sixteen. You?"

"Same," I say. "Where are you?"

"Doesn't matter."

"But I mean, your area code is local. Local to me, I mean."

"I wanted the number to be nearby, I guess."

His voice has flatlined again. The tone makes whatever had drained from my stomach fill right back up again. Acid.

"Why'd you call *this* number?" I say. "Seriously."

"Seriously?" Andrew says. "Seriously, I just figured I should give myself one last shot. Just in case."

"One last shot at what?"

"At . . . God, I don't know. Caring."

"And you want to . . . I mean, you're serious about—doing it?"

"Killing myself? Yeah. Pretty sure. I've pretty much had it. Everything I had . . . everything I *was*. It's just gone."

Andrew's flatline monotone is calm. Maybe too calm. I wonder if it's the same voice Kevin Cooper used to tell his mom good night three months ago. Three months ago *tomorrow*, to be exact.

Or, today, I guess, since it's past midnight. *Ante meridiem?* So it's already the eleventh. When did that happen?

"Are you still there?"

"Yeah," I say. "I'm still here. What have you 'had it' about?"

"Well, I mean . . . I'm alone."

"Why? Where are you?"

"I didn't mean that kind of alone. But I guess I'm that kind too."

"Where are you, like, physically located right now?"

"I really don't want to tell you that."

Aha, I think. Of course you don't, because you don't want me to know where you live and what your real name is!

Except I already told him I was looking up the number on Google, and he didn't react. He couldn't know I don't have a computer right now.

"Why don't you want to tell me where you are?" I say.

"Because I don't want you sending the cops or someone up here to stop me."

Up here? I think. Where on earth . . .

"Oh," I say, and my voice sounds a bit weak. My certainty of him being a prank dips even further.

I swallow dry air. "So, um . . . how?" I ask.

"How, what?"

"How were you planning on . . . doing it?"

Something on his end of the line roars softly. A heartbeat later, I place it: a car engine revving.

"I'm going to let my foot off the brake, slam on the gas, and just fly down this hill and over a cliff," Andrew says. "I don't know if the car will explode or not; I think that's just a Hollywood thing. But I'm pretty high up here, and the drop is pretty far. I think it'll do the trick. The guardrails are for shit. I mean, really, someone could get killed."

He gives that same snort-laugh thing, only this time it's a little heavier on the laugh side.

"Cliff?" I say, and my voice squeaks like our cabinet door.

We're surrounded by mountains, it could be anywhere. Not like the Rockies or anything, but mountains all the same. A twenty-minute drive east of here would put me up two thousand feet or more, at the lake.

If this is a prank call—and it may yet be—it's getting awfully vivid.

"Andrew, if you're screwing around with me . . ."

"*I*," Andrew says emphatically, "have *no* reason. To screw with *you*. Believe that. Vicky, right?"

"Victoria. Tori."

"Believe that, Tori." The engine revs again.

Still suspicious, but also scared of Andrew being legit, I

say, "So what do you expect me to do, here? You won't tell me where you are; I can't send anyone to help you—"

"There isn't anyone, don't you get that?" Andrew says. "That's my whole point. There isn't anyone. Anywhere. Ever. The one person I had is gone and there is no one left."

"Except you dialed a random phone number and got me, so there goes that theory," I say with my own brand of sarcasm. I'm probably not much better at it. Jack's always been the comedian in the family.

When Andrew doesn't respond, I bite my lip. God, if he is serious, then making a joke is the last thing I should do right now.

Didn't I learn that much, at least?

At that moment I hear a semitruck's horn blast past on his end of the line, Doppler-effecting as it races past.

I suddenly get a flawless, imaginary photo of Andrew in my head: his car, some beat-up old hand-me-down, blue, pulled off to the side of the road, no hazards on, no headlights; this late-night trucker comes tooling down the mountain, turns a corner, sees him there, freaks out, yanks the horn.

He really is out there. On some mountain road.

That's a lot of effort for a prank.

"You're right," Andrew says. "*You're* talking to me. For the time being. So I guess technically you are there. Or, here. Around. Whatever. Thanks."

"So you *don't* really think there's no one out there," I say as my fear begins truly to mount. I don't think this conversation is going to be as simple as I thought it would be five minutes ago. "Otherwise you wouldn't have made a call like this."

"I guess I was looking for a miracle," Andrew says, his voice softening.

"You don't need a miracle," I say, unable to help myself. "You just *don't do it*. It's easy. It's easier to *not* do it, in fact."

"You think so, huh?"

"Andrew," I say, lowering my voice, because the last thing I need is Mom barging in here again, "please. I'm asking you— I'm begging you, please, just go home. Okay? I'll even stay on the phone until you get there if you want, if you're really serious about all this."

"You still don't believe me."

I tell myself, *Run these bases cautiously, Victoria Renée. Just in case.*

"I believe you enough that I'll do whatever it takes to get you home safe, yes."

Andrew snort-laughs. "Nice," he says. "See, that's what I meant. There's nobody anywhere who gives a shit about anybody else. That is exactly my point. This isn't about me, Tori. It's about everybody. Everybody screwing everybody else over, and—god, *fuck* this!"

The engine roars.

"Andrew, wait!"

Mom opens my door and sticks her head in.

"Tori? It's late. Get off the phone."

Friend Requests

Lucas Mulcahy	Confirm	Not Now
Albert Jiminez	Confirm	Not Now
Steve Weide	Confirm	Not Now
Delmar Jackson	Confirm	Not Now
Dakota Lorey	Confirm	Not Now

FIVE

"Please, wait!" I plead into the phone.

The engine rev slowly fades. "All right," Andrew says, like he's saying it between closed teeth.

"Thank you," I say, feeling momentarily stupid for it, then turn to face Mom.

"I really can't get off the phone," I say, dropping my arm so the flip is beside my leg.

"Yes, you really can, and you really will," Mom goes, rubbing her temple with two fingers. She does this when she's about ready to explode. It's like she's sending telepathic warning rays to her victims. I figured this out years ago. Jack's still not getting it, and he's nineteen.

She's been doing it a lot lately.

"Mom," I say, as calmly and patiently as I can so I don't set her off about my *tone*, "I swear, this is really important, and I can't hang up right now—"

"Victoria," Mom says, which is warning number two, "I took the last phone and I will take this one too. You're lucky to even have it."

"I know, I know, but Mom . . ."

"God*dammit*!" Jack's voice blares from the kitchen.

Eesh. I think I know what that's about. The coffeemaker. Right.

Mom winces and turns to glance out my doorway, as if that will somehow enable her magical mom eyeballs to go down the hall, turn, and enter the kitchen of their own accord. Then again, maybe they can. Moms are kind of superpowered that way, like Jack's X-Men or whoever. One of the worst parts of this whole mess is that Mom and Dad couldn't just make it all go away, like when I lost a game or did poorly on a test.

What do you do when your parents look as scared as you feel?

"Oh, now what?" Mom groans, and, dismissing me entirely, tightens the belt on her robe and leaves, heading for the kitchen.

Mom would get a lot more done in life if she didn't micromanage her kids. Now is probably not the time to suggest it.

I hurry to my door and shut it softly, grateful that Jack, even in his idiocy and silent treatment, has managed to bail me out.

"Are you still there?" I say into the phone when my latch has shut.

Nothing.

"Andrew?"

I press a hand to my other ear, listening as hard as I can. I'm pretty sure I can hear the rain still.

"Andy," his voice says at last.

"Are you okay?"

"I'm fine. Thanks for asking. Can you call me Andy?"

Will you kill yourself if I don't? I think, and squeeze my eyes shut. I came way too close to blurting that out. Someone should suture my mouth shut. If they used red thread, my whole face could look like a softball, ready to be batted into the outfield.

"Andy, sure," I say, and sit on my bed, blowing out a breath.

"You sound relieved."

"I *am*."

"That I'm alive?"

He says it in a challenging way. And it's too late, and I'm too tired, and too much is going wrong for me to try to be all nicey-nice about this.

"Yes!" I say. "I'm relieved you're alive. Isn't that what this is all about? That someone cares? There, I've said it."

"Wow," Andy says. "I'm not sure whether to feel grateful or, you know, *suicidal* after that."

I laugh.

Just once, one little bark of a thing, which quickly trans-
forms into a sob that I punch back down my throat before it can
come out.

But he laughs too. Also just once, or maybe twice, short
and sharp.

Then we're both quiet.

"You mind if I ask what you look like, Tori?" Andy says
after a minute.

I feel my eyebrows rise. So all this, and it's just *phone sex*
he's after?

On the other hand, no pun intended, maybe that wouldn't
be the worst thing in the world right now, even if it's totally
gross. It's better than if he's telling the truth about the cliff anyway. I could definitely hang up then.

"Why?" I ask him.

"Just so I can get an image in my head."

Yep. So this whole suicide thing, just a ruse for a perv looking for a virtual hookup.

"I don't think so," I say.

"Why not?" Andy says, then immediately afterward, goes,
"Oh! Sorry. No. That probably sounds like . . . Yeah, that didn't
come out right at all. God. How the hell do I make it through
the day, y'know?"

He sounds genuine. Okay. I'll let it slide.

"Longer hair," I say, taking my time. "Past my shoulders. I
usually wear it back, though. . . ."

The truth is, and I'm okay with this, there's not much

remarkable about me. I tend to blend in. I don't think I'm ugly, but I don't think I'm cute. Even my hair is an everyday brown. Shiny, maybe, but just sort of thick and straight and—I don't know—unassuming?

I mean, is it any wonder that Lucas might have an eye on other people beside me? If he has an eye on me at all.

"Nice," Andy says. Sounds like he forced himself to say it, though, like he's still reeling from sounding like a creeper.

"Yeah?" I ask. "Why's that?"

"I just think it's . . . I dunno. Cool. Like that. Pulled back, I mean. I like it when girls pull their hair back." He breathes out, once, harsh. "I am making no sense at all."

I get a very clear picture of *him* right then. No way to prove it, of course, and I don't particularly feel like asking him what he looks like, but, somehow, I know.

Black hair. Long.

Kind of skinny. And tall.

A long, hooked nose and high-as-hell cheekbones.

Brown eyes. I want to imagine them blue but can't. I think that's what makes me so sure my imagination is right; otherwise, I could make them any color I wanted.

He's sitting with his hand draped over the steering wheel of his . . .

His—

"So what kind of car you driving?" I ask. Maybe he'll slip up, give me a clue about where he is.

"A Sentra," Andy says.

"Yeah? What color?"

"White. Plain, boring white."

Interesting. I don't know why I'd figured blue. I'm not going to tell him this, though.

"It's my mom's," Andy goes on. "She'd . . . heh."

"What?"

"I was just gonna say, 'She'd kill me if she knew what I was going to do with it,' but I guess that wouldn't really matter, huh?"

I lick my lips. My tongue feels like a sandpaper caterpillar. This is my first real clue.

"Are there any . . . you know, like, landmarks nearby?"

He's not buying it. "Tori, you can't stop me like that."

"Like what?"

"There's no time for you to come up here and talk me down," Andy says. "Or send a hostage negotiator or whatever. It's just you and me."

He makes a noise like he's stretching. Must be cramped, sitting in that car seat.

"So whaddya got?" Andy says.

I try to lick my lips again and only dry them out even more. Andy's smart. Smart enough to know what I was thinking, anyway. Not that I was being particularly subtle. And, again—he's right. Even if I borrowed one of my parents' or Jack's cars, or tried to get ahold of the police, he could be down that hill and over the cliff in a matter of seconds.

But what hill? Where?

I guess it doesn't matter. What could I possibly tell the cops? Why would they believe me?

More to the point, why would they believe *me* in particular? I wouldn't if I were them.

"What do I got, what?" I say, stupidly.

"Tell me why not," Andy says. "Tell me why I shouldn't do it. Give me one reason why I shouldn't drive my mom's Sentra over this cliff in a nice big blaze of teenage angst and glory."

"I don't know," I say, then shake my head. Not a great reason, there. "I mean, because you're young, what about that?"

"Since when is being young so wonderful?" Andy says. "Seems like a twenty-year cruel joke some Flying Spaghetti Monster dreamed up to make us miserable so we'd be better prepared for even *more* misery after we got out of college."

"Wait," I say. "A flying *what*?"

"Flying Spaghetti Monster. You never heard of that?"

I run through a mental catalog of SpongeBob cartoons. "No."

"It's an atheist term for God. It's like, believing in God makes as much sense as believing in the Flying Spaghetti Monster."

"Oh."

"Do you believe in God?"

Wait a second, I think. This is the second time he's asked me that. Is that what this really is? Is this some whacked-out cult calling people at all hours to get them to drink the magic Kool-Aid or whatever?

And what the hell does that expression even mean, any-way? Maybe it's something to do with whatever religion Tom Cruise is.

No. It seems unlikely. Of course, so does a suicidal guy ran-domly calling my number.

I need help. In more ways than one, ha. No, really, I can't handle Andy on my own.

"Um, God?" I say to Andy, while weighing my options. Who can give me a hand here?

My mind goes straight to Jack, my big bro, who until this whole mess went down never failed to back me up or defend me, even if he is a gigantic dork. Now that I've apparently ruined his entire life for all eternity—and hey, Bro, mine's no picnic right now, you ever think of that?—there's not much chance he would help me out. He's made that clear.

"Yep," Andy says. "The big man upstairs himself. What's your take?"

"Overrated and underappreciated."

"Aren't you underappreciating him by virtue of calling him overrated?"

"Well, sure, why not. I'm a very complicated person."

"That doesn't surprise me."

There's Noah, of course. He's reliable. More than reli-able, I mean. We've been friends for so long now, and he's the only person who's come by the house. He said it was to trade some anime movies with Jack, but he stayed and talked to me for more than an hour. He's probably still up, doing his chat thing. How can I get ahold of him when Andy's on my phone? God, this whole not-connected thing is going to drive me insa—

"Wait, what?" I say. "What do you mean, that doesn't surprise you?"

"You, um—sound like someone who has a lot on her mind," Andy says after a moment. "Distracted."

"It's that obvious, huh?"

"A bit. What's going on?"

I shake my head again, again realizing it's a stupid gesture since he can't see me. "Absolutely nothing that I want to get into. Plus, you're the one who's . . . you know."

"Yeah, but I asked you to tell me why I shouldn't 'you know,' and so far you've given me a bunch of crap about being young. I want to know what you think about God. So do you?"

Now I'm confused. "Do I what?"

"Do you believe in God?"

"I don't know anymore," I say. "I don't know what to believe. I hope I still do. So I guess I did at some point."

"And now?"

"Now I think that even if he does exist, he doesn't give much of a crap what happens down here."

"Ah," Andy says, like this makes perfect sense. "Me too. Used to, I mean. My family was never real big on church or anything, just holidays, you know? I always thought it was hypocritical to go to church just twice a year."

"You mean like Easter and Christmas?"

"Nah, in our family it was Groundhog Day and Take Your Daughter to Work Day."

It's not a hysterical joke, but I laugh just a bit. Even though Andy doesn't make a sound, I feel like he smiles.

"Kidding," Andy says, like I didn't know that. "Yeah, we only went on Christmas and Easter. I mean, come on, if God's really out there somewhere, he's only popping his head in the doors at church to make sure you're coming to the big holidays? What kind of God is that?"

"A very bored one," I say. "Actually, it sounds a little like my mom. She does that too. Sticking her head in the door, I mean."

Andy laughs. Not much, but it's a laugh. Bigger than the snort-cough thing. That's good, right? That's a good sign, isn't it?

My door flies open. I squeal and fall back onto my bed. Jack stands in the door, pulling on a light jacket over his Target-brand graphic T-shirt. Sometimes I want to take him shopping for real clothes.

"Thanks for the coffee, Vic" is all he says, and he disappears down the hall. A moment later I hear the front door open and close before I can even think to tell him it just needs to be plugged back in.

"Great," I say.

"What was that?" Andy says.

"My brother. I ruined his night. No, wait, his life, according to him."

"Yeah? How'd you do that?"

"Nothing, forget it."

"Family does indeed suck from time to time," Andy says, but it sounds like it's almost to himself.

I can't hear Jack's car, but I see his headlights sweep across my window through the shades. He's probably going to 7-Eleven for coffee now. Must have a big paper due or something; otherwise, I don't think he'd be up this late. Jack's kind of square that way except for the whole Internet-porn thing.

Internet . . .

Laptop!

"Could you, um, hold on for just a sec?" I say to Andy. "Or maybe a minute or two?"

"How come?"

"I need to . . . go to the bathroom."

"Take me with you. I won't listen."

"Seriously, I don't talk to people in the bathroom. It's really freaky."

"Now I'm freaky," Andy says. "No surprise there."

"Wait, no, that's not what I said. I just—it's a thing. Okay? Will you be okay just for a minute or two?"

Andy is quiet. I'm already heading down the hall.

"Yeah," he says. "Sure."

"Thanks," I say, and slip the phone into my pocket.

Tori Hershberger UGH. Sometimes life just sucks.

Like · Comment · Share · April 3, one year ago

👍2 people like this.

Kevin Cooper I hear ya. whats your story?

👍You like this.

Marly DeSoto you break a nail Cooper?

👍You and 4 others like this.

Lucas Mulcahy haha marly. whats up tori?

👍You like this.

Tori Hershberger Hey, Lucas! Great game last night. How many homers is that?

👍2 people like this.

Lucas Mulcahy four. whats up

👍You like this.

Tori Hershberger I probably hate probability problems. :)

Kevin Cooper You need help?

Tori Hershberger I got it. Thanks.

Lucas Mulcahy math is for pussies!!

Kevin Cooper Math put men on the moon

Lucas Mulcahy pussy

SIX

I open Jack's door. The light's still on, which means he definitely isn't going to be gone long. How much time do I have?
Assuming he went only as far as 7-Eleven to get coffee, ten
minutes, tops. But maybe that's enough.

I open the laptop and hit the power button. Jack's desktop screen is—jaw-dropping surprise—a scantily clad woman.
And she's only scantily clad in case someone should happen
to see his desktop; otherwise, I'm sure she'd be totally naked.
Gross. This particular princess is riding what appears to be
a tyrannosaurus dragon. Geek check. No wonder Jack never
made any friends in high school besides guys like Noah.
Gamers and anime freaks and whatnot. He's such a dork.

I open his browser and log in to my Gmail account, hoping
against hope. But for once this month, things go my way. Noah
is logged in too. I open a chat window.

> **Me:** Noah!
> **Noah:** Tori-chan!!! where are you? howd you
> get a computer?
> **Me:** It's Jack's. This guy just called me and
> says he

I stop typing.

How exactly should I finish this little sentence? Noah may still be talking to me, even supporting me, but even though he's totally been on my side through the whole thing, is it fair to drag him into something else now?

Whatever. I need help. And he's never let me down.

I finish typing:

> is going to kill himself.
> **Noah:** huh???
> **Me:** You've got to believe me, he's on the phone
> right now!
> **Noah:** who is it?
> **Me:** He says his name is Andy. Do you know
> anyone named Andy or Andrew?
> **Noah:** no. whyd he call you?
> **Me:** He said it was at random.
> **Noah:** wow thats got to be a total lie
> **Me:** I know! But I think he might really mean it.
> I can't risk it if he is serious. I have to help him
> somehow.

I don't bother correcting my typo. Normally I'm a perfectionist about that kind of thing. Even online. No time to worry about it now.

> **Noah:** its probably someone from school
> messing with you again. that sucks.
> **Me:** I thought so too at first, but now I don't
> know. You have to help me okay?
> **Noah:** totally. how?

I hesitate, trying to come up with a reasonable and feasible answer. Instead, I end up writing the truth.

> **Me:** I don't know.

The kitchen door opens. My brother's back.

Without thinking, I grab his laptop and rush to my room, closing the door and locking it behind me. Like that'll do any good. He's going to see that it's gone, come knocking on my door and shouting, wake up our parents. . . .

I take my phone out and set it on the nightstand and put my brother's computer where mine used to sit.

> **Me:** I don't have much time. Can you come over
> and meet me outside or something?
> **Noah:** wow ok. knock your window maybe?
> **Me:** yes cool thank you!!!

Again, now's not the time to show off my perfect English skills.

I hear keys jingling in the kitchen as Jack hangs them on the pegboard beside the door, and a second later his bedroom door closes. Ticktock, ticktock.

> **Noah:** I'll come to your window
> **Me:** Okay.

Thump. Thump. Thump.

Three distinct, muffled, and angry knocks on my door. Cursing, I get up and open the door.

"Please," I say to Jack right away.

"Stay out of my room, Victoria," Jack says between clenched teeth. "And give me my computer back."

"I'll do anything," I say, because at this point, I really will. The laptop, the Internet, is too valuable right now. I actually *could* Google Andy's number, find out who he really is maybe, for starters.

"Anything?" Jack asks me.

"Yes!" I say quickly.

"Okay, then," Jack says.

I'm stupid enough to have hope for just one moment, which ends as Jack continues: "Shut your mouth and give me my stuff back!"

"I'll scream," I try. "I'll wake up Mom and Dad." This used to work when we were younger.

Jack laughs, cold. "Please do," he says. "I can't wait to tell them you broke into my room and stole my computer so you could go online, where they specifically told you not to go anymore. Scream away, Vic."

Reflexively, I punch him in the arm for calling me Vic. He punches me back. We start a stare down.

I actually win the stare down, but only because Jack relaxes and leans against my doorframe. "Do you want to hand it to me, or do you want me to knock you over and go get it myself? Your call."

Fuming, I hiss back at him, "Fine."

Even though I'm athletic and Jack is decidedly not, he's got that Big Brother gene that allows him to win all physical confrontations. I stomp over to my bed, slap the laptop shut, and give it back to Jack. He takes it without a word and goes back down the hall. I shut my door and drop onto my bed, picking up the phone.

"Andy?"

No response.

"Andrew?"

Nothing.

Oh, God.

Kevin Cooper wrote on your timeline.
April 30, one year ago.
So those are your new friends huh?

Like · Comment · Share

👍Noah Murphy likes this.

Tori Hershberger Relax, Kevin. They're nice.

Lucas Mulcahy What's that sperm bank Cooper talking about tori?

👍You and 4 others like this.

Marly DeSoto ouch, cruel Lucas! but also true so . . .

👍You and 4 others like this.

Tori Hershberger It's cool, everyone. :)

Noah Murphy I think you mean cold

SEVEN

"Andy? Andy, come on. Be there. Andy? Hello?"

Rustling.

"Hello?" Andy says. "Tori?"

I clutch my throat with my free hand, amazed at the speed of my pulse. "You scared me," I say.

"Sorry," Andy says. "I figured I should use the facilities too. My facilities ended up being a bush, though. So what were you writing about?"

"Huh?"

"Are you writing a book or something?" Andy asks. "You're a loud typer."

Oh, great. I hadn't thought to mute the phone. "No! No, just . . . um . . . blogging."

I wince. That sounds awful. I'm used to physical reflexes, not mental ones.

"Wow," Andy says slowly. "My life is in your hands and you're recording the whole experience for posterity. That's terrific. You sound like a real gem, Tori."

"I've been called worse," I say.

"Oh yeah? Like what?"

"Bitch. Monster. Oh, evil homophobic slut bomb was a personal favorite. Murd—uh, jerk. Stuff like that. So, yeah, 'gem' doesn't really have any cutting power."

"What was that one in the middle?" Andy asks. "Turd?"

"Um . . . yeah. Something like that."

"That must keep you up nights," Andy says. "People out there calling you a turd."

"I'm over it."

"Who's doing it?" he asks. "Who's calling you that stuff?"

"Why, you going to protect me?"

"If I make it through the night, I might."

Cute. I can't even count the number of ways I don't want to get into this with him. With anyone. So I say, "Thanks. It's nobody in particular."

"Is it people at school?" Andy presses. "Or, like, online or something?"

"Sure, yeah," I say quickly.

"Sucks, doesn't it?" Andy says, and his voice has gotten softer. "People calling you names like that."

"You could say that." I stop and consider for a second. "Is that what happened to you? I mean, people talking shit?"

"It *has* happened," Andy says. "But is that what parked me

at the top of a hill overlooking the city? No, not exactly. I'm not *that* big of a nancy."

"Okay," I say carefully, and peek through my blinds, as if Noah could've gotten here in two minutes. "So what, then? How'd you end up—here?"

Andy is silent. And a heartbeat later that silence is filled by three thumps on my door.

"Crap, hold on," I say quickly into the phone, and go open the door.

Jack stands there with the laptop resting on his upturned arm. He flips it toward me, showing the chat window with Noah that I, of course, did not close. Like I said, I'm not a fast thinker.

"What the hell is this?" Jack says, turning the screen back toward himself, scowling and underlit by the white light from his screen.

"I tried to tell you," I say in a harsh whisper, and then remember to hit the mute button on my phone. "You didn't care."

"You mean someone really called you to say they were going to commit suicide?"

"Yes! I told you that."

"And they're not kidding?"

"Oh, gee, Jack, I never thought of that, let me ask him."

Jack considers this for a moment. It's long enough for me to realize that this is the most we've talked in a month. Ever since Dad told him they might have to raid his college account to pay for Mr. Halpern if my account isn't enough.

"You think he means it," Jack says finally, as if my sarcasm was totally lost on him. Maybe it was.

I lean against my door frame. "I don't know," I say. "Probably not. I mean, what are the chances, right?"

Jack snorts, and, very quickly, a look of pure disgust passes over his face. It makes my heart shrivel.

"But so far, he sounds for real," I go on. "I don't know."

"Where is he?"

"Some hill. Outside. One of the mountains, I guess, on a highway I think. I heard one of those tractor-trailer horns going by."

"That's all you got?"

"Yeah. Jack, please, you've got to help me. If something happens, if he's really serious and something bad happens, and he has my number on his cell . . ."

"How'd he get your number?"

"Says he dialed it randomly."

"You believe that?"

"Not exactly. But I don't have any choice."

Jack snorts again. "You got that right." Suddenly Jack shakes his head and backs off. "Well, good luck," he says.

"Wait!" I whisper-screech. "Can't you at least let me borrow your laptop?"

"No."

"Jack!"

"What?"

"Come on! At least let me look up his number!"

Jack shakes his head again, melodramatically walking backward down the hall toward his door. "No," he repeats. "This is your mess, Vic. Maybe you should figure a way out of it. Or maybe try, I dunno, helping the guy out. Be a nice change of pace."

"I can help him if you let me use your laptop, dumb-ass!" I say, following him into the hallway.

"Right, because I have satellite-imaging capabilities and just so happened to plant a tracking device on this guy too. Brilliant."

"I can at least look up his number and see if it matches the name he gave me," I say. "That way if he's lying, I can go to sleep."

"And that helps *him* somehow, right?"

I clench about three dozen fists. "Goddammit, Jack!"

"It's still all about you, isn't it?" Jack says. "Jesus, Vic. Why can't you just assume he's for real? Why can't you just offer to listen or to talk him down, or whatever needs to be done?"

"Because *I'm on fucking trial*, Jack," I whisper, and it sounds demonic.

He's not impressed. I never could scare him. "All the more reason to stick with him, even if he's full of crap," Jack says. "If it's a sick joke, you lose a little sleep. If it's not, maybe you can—"

He cuts himself off, snapping his mouth closed. I peer at him in the dark hallway, trembling at the many, many ways that sentence might end.

"Maybe I can what?"

My big brother stares at me. For a long time. Then he snorts and shakes his head. "My computer can't help you help him," Jack says. "You're gonna have to do that on your own. If you want to."

"If I want to?" I say. "What is that supposed to mean?"

"Oh, now suddenly you don't remember Jack *Pus*-Berger? Krakatoa? Cyst—"

These are all names Jack got called during the worst of his acne. I interrupt him. "What does any of that have to do with this?"

Jack narrows his eyes. "I was an inconvenience to you last year," he says. "And that's the only way you could see me. Well, now this guy's inconveniencing *you*. Oh, snap."

But Jack's sarcasm flies past me. Or, *through* me, maybe.

"You think that's what I thought about you?" I say. "That you were an inconvenience?"

"If I had a dollar for every time you talked to me at school last year, Victoria," Jack says, "I'd have about a buck fifty."

"*You* didn't talk to *me!*"

"If I didn't talk to you, it was because you were too busy with your little jock buddies," Jack says. "And look what hanging out with *them* got you."

Trust me: If I could call Jack a liar right now, I would. In an instant. I have no trouble telling him when he's full of it. What I've never been very good at, though, is refuting him when he's telling the truth.

Jack doesn't give me time to form a response. "Better get back to your call," he says, and continues on toward his room.

I shake my head to snap back to my immediate issue. "At least let me Google the number, Jack. Please?"

Jack pauses, then turns to me, gritting his teeth. "Gimme the phone."

I go grab it and show him the screen. He types the number in while the laptop is still balanced on his arm. He scans the page.

"Nothing," he says. "It's a cell, and it's local. If you want to know who it is, you'd need a credit card."

"Would you—"

"No. It doesn't *matter*," Jack says, clearly impatient. "Knowing if he is who he says he is doesn't help *him*. Look, just stay up with him. All night if you have to. Things will look better when the sun comes up."

"But the hearing . . ."

"Somehow I'm sure Mom and Dad will make sure you're there on time. I gotta get back to work."

"Are you coming tomorrow?" I blurt.

Jack hesitates, and doesn't look at me.

"I don't know," he mumbles.

With that, he finishes his walk to his room and closes the door behind him.

Feeling my body go empty, I go back to my room and close my door too, and put the phone back to my ear. I've got to get my head back in the game. Basically, Jack is right; whether

Andy is lying or not has nothing to do with him and everything to do with me. I want to sleep just so I don't look like a
burnout tomorrow morning in court. Right now, this is more
important.

"Sorry," I say to Andy after tapping the mute button off. "It
was my brother again." I try to erase Jack's voice playing on
repeat in my head. *I don't know. I don't know.*

"It's okay," Andy says, and he sounds tired. "No big. You
love him?"

"Who, Jack? My brother?" I sit down on the edge of my bed
and hunch my shoulders. "Now is maybe not the best time to
ask. I mean, fundamentally, yes. I do. It's just that lately he's
been a real bitch."

"Why lately?"

The real reasons spring to mind, but I'm not about to talk
to Andy about them. And without stopping to consider why
I'm telling him anything at all, I say, "Some of my friends used
to make fun of him a little, and he thinks it's my fault or something."

"Is it?"

"What? No! Wait a sec, you're the one on the verge of offing
himself and you're going to psychoanalyze *me*?"

Andy laughs a bit. "Sure. Why not." He affects a deeper,
professional voice. "Tell me about your parents."

Smirking, I just say, "Whatever."

"No, really," Andy says. "What about them? Do you love
them?"

I shift my position. "Getting awful personal there, aren't you?"

Andy's momentary jokey mood ends abruptly. "I got nothing to lose," he says.

Right, I think. *Of course not.*

"I love them, yeah," I say.

More comes to mind, but I don't say it. The truth is, I know my parents love me. They're mad right now. Sure. Why not? I guess I would be too. But I know they love me. I wish my whole stupid thing hadn't happened so they wouldn't have to go through all this. I wish that for Jack, too. I mean, he didn't do anything wrong. Except maybe be a huge nerd, ha-ha.

"They still married?" Andy asks me.

"Yeah."

"Wow," he says. "Who'd've thunk it was still possible?"

I laugh—a very, very little—despite myself. "Yours?"

"Not anymore."

"Recently?"

"Nah. A while back."

"I'm sorry."

"No worries."

"No worries" is something of an understatement considering where you are and what you are doing, I think, but have the intelligence not to say. But only barely.

"Is that why you're out there?" I ask anyway.

"Not exactly."

"So then why?"

Andy sighs, but it's not all showy like mine are. Like one of those nasal sighs.

"You really want to know?"

"All things considered, it's the least you can do."

Andy hesitates. "All right," he says. "Fine. But it's just a bunch of sappy romantic horseshit likely to make your ears bleed."

I lie back on my mattress. "Don't take this the wrong way," I say, "but that sounds pretty good right now."

Andy grunts. Maybe it was another weird laugh.

"All right," he says. "This is what happened."

Kevin Cooper life is one giant fucking toilet bowl. and no one ever flushes. shit just piles up and piles up until it gets clogged. it doesn't go anywhere. it just sits and rots and smells

Like · Comment · Share · May 6, one year ago

Tori Hershberger Super Duper Pooper Cooper? :)

Kevin Cooper No tori I'm fucking serious.

Tori Hershberger What's going on?

Kevin Cooper Can I just text you

👍Noah Murphy likes this.

Tori Hershberger Maybe later. I really need to study. Hang in there, okay?

EIGHT

"Her name was Kayla," Andy says.

"Uh-huh?" I say.

"We met at—"

Thump, thump, thump.

Dammit, Jack . . .

"Uh, hold on again," I say, and get up.

Jack is waiting impatiently when I open my door. He shoves his laptop toward me.

"It's Noah," he says.

Juggling the phone while trying to keep my thumb over the receiver and take the laptop from Jack is something of a chore.

"You didn't log me out?" I demand.

"Why didn't you log yourself out, genius?"

"Because you came barging in here before I could!"

"What possible interest could your stupid e-mail hold for me?"

"I don't know, looking for sexy softball team pictures maybe?"

"I'd consider that if any of you were sexy."

At a loss, I resort to a withering glare.

Jack, knowing he's scored a point, jabs a finger toward me. "I'm making Pop-Tarts!" he declares, which actually does make me laugh out loud. God, I've got to learn to control myself. "When I'm done, I want my computer back and that's it. Got it?"

Several smart-ass responses come to mind, but since he just loaned me the laptop, I can't exactly use any of them.

"Yes, yes," I say to him, and drop to my knees, setting the laptop on my bed. I drop the phone on the mattress and quickly open the chat window.

Noah's message reads:

> **Noah:** Are you still there? I'm going to have to sneak out and find a way to get the car without anyone noticing.

Crap. I write back:

> **Me:** What about your bike?
> **Noah:** Flat. You want me to hoof it?
> **Me:** If that's what it takes. I owe you big-time.
> **Noah:** Yep. :) OK I'm leaving now.
> **Me:** THANK YOU NOAH!

Something crackles over the flip phone. Andy's still there. He's saying something. I pick the phone back up.

"Sorry, I had to . . . deal with my brother. What'd you say?"

"I said, you're still typing," Andy says.

"Listen," I say, "you have my full attention, I swear to God. I just . . . I'm taking notes, okay?"

"Notes? I'm not giving a pop quiz after this."

"Notes on everything you're saying, everything I'm saying. I have to cover my ass here. I hope you understand that."

Andy's voice gets suspicious. "Cover your ass, how?"

At that, I get pissed. I stand up from the carpet and damn near throw the phone right through my door and into the kitchen.

Which, oddly, reminds me suddenly that I'm actually hungry. I check the time. 1:38 a.m. You know what sounds good right now? Steak. A steak burrito, never mind chicken. Steak burrito with everything. There's a twenty-four-hour Mexican food place a few blocks from here. If only my parents would let me drive again. If only it weren't after one thirty in the morning.

If only I weren't on the phone with a suicidal freak show.

"I'm covering my ass in case I wake up tomorrow morning and find out some dude drove his car off a cliff and I was the last person to talk to him!" I whisper in a way that sounds very much like screaming.

Andy's quiet. Still there, I'm sure. But quiet.

"This is stupid," he whispers finally.

I rub my eyes. "No, no, you're not stupid, come on."

"*This* is stupid. I didn't say *I* was stupid."

"Well, either way."

"I shouldn't have called you. That was the stupid thing. I'm sorry. I should—"

"You woulda done it already," I blurt.

Another silence.

Oh, God. No, no, no, Tori, you complete idiot. . . .

"What?" Andy says. He sounds pissed now. Pissed, or maybe shocked.

I try to swallow but only choke on air. "You don't want to commit . . . you know. *Do* this. You would've already done it if you really wanted to. You know?"

I hear him snort. It reminds me of Jack. Which irritates me.

"You don't know anything about me," Andy says.

I can hear Jack's voice in my head. *Stay up with him. All night if you have to. Things will look better when the sun comes up.* "Okay, so, tell me," I say. "I'm here. I'm listening."

"No, you're not, you're blogging."

"I'm not blogging," I say. "I'm just . . . writing some stuff down, is all."

"Stuff about me?"

"Both of us. I just told you."

"Well. I'm flattered."

It occurs to me that I've actually got the right idea: I should be keeping a record of this in case something bad happens to Andy. *Document everything*, Mr. Halpern said. *Even if you don't think it's important, document everything.* When the brick smashed Mom's car window, Mr. Halpern made us all write down what we knew about it. Which wasn't much. Probably whoever threw it picked Mom's car because it was parked on the street and was easier to hit. It could have been anyone's car. All that mattered was that it was in front of my house.

The chat with Noah will be archived automatically, so that's something. Plus, my phone and Andy's phone will show that *he* called *me* first, proof I didn't initiate contact. That might be important if he—

You know.

"I get it," Andy goes on. "It's okay. Keeping a record probably makes sense. I guess I'm really screwing up your night, huh?"

"You could say that."

When Andy laughs, it catches me completely off guard. This guy's mood has more swings than a playground. That's probably not a sign of good mental health.

"I really am pissing you off, aren't I," he says.

Would a suicidal guy really laugh? Unless he's already made up his mind to go through with it, and all this is just some sick psycho thing he's doing.

"Do you really think this is funny?" I say.

His laugh cuts short. "No."

"Good," I say. "Because I don't either."

"You're not really writing all this down, are you," Andy says, kind of all of a sudden, and not like a question. "You're not typing when I'm talking. . . . Are you chatting with someone? Is that it?"

"No!"

Oh yeah, *that* sounded believable.

"Who is it, Tori? Don't screw around with me."

The car engine revs.

"It's no one—I mean, I'm not, no."

Worst. Liar. Ever.

The engine sound dies down. "Oh, I get it," Andy says. "You got a boyfriend? And now he's all jealous over little old me?"

"He's not my boyfriend," I say.

"Ah," Andy says. "So who is he?"

"Just a friend. His name's Noah."

"Yeah? Is he hot?"

"Why, you want me to hook you two up or what?"

Andy laughs. It's about the most genuine laugh I've heard from him thus far. "No, that's okay," he says.

"What about Kayla? Was she hot?"

"What?"

"Your girlfriend," I say. "Was she hot?"

Andy goes silent for a few seconds. "I guess," he says. "I didn't think of her that way, though. I mean, I didn't think of her exclusively in terms of how attractive she was. That's not why I liked her."

He hesitates.

"So you and this Noah guy . . ."

"I'm not dating Noah."

"Well, that's what you say, but—"

"No, I mean, even if I wanted to, I wouldn't. He's my friend. It would be weird."

"Ah," Andy says. "Okay. So then is there someone else?"

"Why?"

"Because the story I'm going to tell you is a bit on the dark side," Andy says, and I think, *Surprise, surprise.* "I want to know where you stand with relationships. You're not seeing someone now?"

I blow a hair out of my face. "Not for lack of trying, I guess."

"Yeah? So you're crushing on someone?"

"I was." *I am*, is more like the truth, but with each day passing that I don't get to see or talk to Lucas, I worry that any chance I *might* have had is slipping.

"What happened?" Andy asks.

"I thought you wanted to talk about your girlfriend."

"I thought you said you'd do whatever it took to get me home safe."

This is a mind game. There's no doubt about it, as far as I'm concerned, but, dammit, I can't figure out what it is, and I can't risk just hanging up. I feel like I'm a teller at a bank robbery and the robber only has a note saying he'll kill a baby or something if I don't hand over the money.

Hostage. That's what I am. A hostage.

"Yes," I say, rubbing my eyes. "That's true. Whatever it takes."

"I appreciate that," Andy says, and his voice sort of changes for a second, like he's shifting his sitting position or something.

"So tell me about this guy you like. What's his name?"

Great.

"Lucas," I say.

"Uh-*huh*, and where do you *know* him from . . . ?" Andy sings, like he's having a grand old time.

"School."

"He like you back?"

"I don't know."

"Ah, you haven't told him yet."

"Not exactly. I was hoping to, but."

"But?"

"Some things came up." Being charged with felonies has that effect, but I don't say it to Andy.

"What do you like about him?"

"He plays baseball," I say, trying hard not to let my voice go all gooey-girlie. "He's really good. And his arms are just . . . yeah."

"Huh," Andy says. "So he's a good-looking young chappie."

"Yeah," I say. "He is. It's true."

"But what else?"

"What else, what?"

"What else do you like about him? Please don't tell me it's all about his looks or the fact that he's some sporto hero."

"I just . . . like him," I say. And it sounds stupid. I can hear it in my own voice.

"I'm disappointed," Andy says. "I'd expect you to go after someone who believed in truth, justice, the American way, all that stuff. But he's just a pretty face, huh?"

I squeeze my eyelids shut for a long moment to try to get some moisture back into them.

"Maybe," I say. But what I think is, *I don't know. Is he?* I mean, when I've gone out with that group, like up to the lake, I felt like more of an initiate than a member. The JV team, sort of. Like they were trying me out. I'm not blind; I've seen how Lucas is around the other girls, even my teammates. But they didn't get invited to the lake, or to Lucas and Marly's table for lunch. That's not my fault. And I'm pretty sure that if I was to throw myself at him—you know, *open wide*—he wouldn't hesitate to take it.

I don't want that. I want everything: talking and laughing and hanging out, *plus* kissing and all the rest of it.

"Well, you should tell him," Andy says. "If he's just eye candy, you got nothing to lose."

"Yeah, I guess. I don't know." I hate that I'm even thinking about this. My whole life is going to change tomorrow. Lucas Mulcahy should be the last thing I'm worried about. But then, shouldn't that be true for Andy, too?

"Tori, let me tell you something, as I sit up here looking at the stars above this back-asswards little town and into the gloom of certain death just down the highway from me," Andy says, and for some reason, I visualize his eyes closing, not open.

"Okay?" I say.

"Life is short," Andy says. "Am I right?"

I answer cautiously, "Yes . . ."

"You should make a move. As soon as possible. You never know what tomorrow's going to bring."

"Yeah. Guess so."

"You sound tired, Tori."

"Listen," I say, "please don't get upset or anything, okay? But why are you doing this? I don't want anything to happen to you, okay? I really don't. But if you sincerely did just call me at random, how come? Because I'm really confused about what the hell it is we're talking about here. Why are you asking me about Lucas?"

Andy is quiet for a second. When he speaks, his voice is all business again. Firm. The fun-loving tone he had while asking about Lucas has evaporated into nothing.

"All right," he says. "This fine evening, after pulling off to the side of the road, I was just about to shove the gas pedal down as hard as I could, and instead, I got this idea that if— and this is a big *if*, all right?—if there is a God, or even a Flying Spaghetti Monster, and he didn't want me to die, then I'd just dial a number, and if someone answered, someone who then bothered to give a single, solitary droplet of shit about me, then maybe I wouldn't do it. That's pretty much it, sweetheart. So you're the lucky girl, and so fucking help me, I'm happy to get off this phone any time you want and finish the job."

His tone is so bitter and harsh that it chokes me like a mouthful of baseline chalk.

"Okay," I cough. "Can I ask you something else?"

"Sure." It comes out like a bark, teeth bared.

"Why this way? I mean, why not take pills or something? It'd hurt a lot less."

Andy is quiet again for a minute. "Thing is," he says, and sounds like he's back in control of himself, "it was kind of a spur-of-the-moment decision."

That sounds promising. If he hasn't been planning it, then maybe he isn't committed to going through with it.

"I realized," Andy goes on, "that, for one thing, it wouldn't hurt, not really. No more than a gunshot would, anyway. And pills, someone could stop me. Find me before they finished me off. And this way, nobody else gets hurt."

"How would someone else get hurt any other way?"

"I just mean that this way, it could be an accident," Andy says. "No one would ever know I did it on purpose."

"Except me."

"Well, yes. Except you. Sorry."

Great.

"What you said before," Andy goes. "About my ill-fated romance. You really don't mind listening? Because like I said, it gets a little sappy."

I check the clock. Holy crud, it's after two. Except . . . I don't yawn.

"I'm all ears," I tell him.

"Promise?" Andy says.

"Promise."

"You a woman of your word?"

"Uh . . . I think so."

"Way to inspire confidence, there."

"Look," I tell him, "I'll do whatever it takes to keep you from doing what you said you were going to do."

"You're having a hard time with the word 'suicide,' Tori."

"Well, yeah. Sorry."

Thankfully, he skips asking for clarification. "Will you promise not to ask if I'm serious again?"

"You can trust me."

"I can trust you, huh?" Andy says, like there's a smirk on his face. "Trust you with my life?"

"Well, I mean, I'd rather you didn't have to," I say, honestly enough. "I'd really rather you just said, 'Thanks, I feel better now,' and then drive home."

"I can't do that, Tori. I really can't."

"Why not?" I ask him, trying for a logical tone this time. "Why not just go home and get some sleep? Maybe you'll feel better in the morning. You could talk to your parents, or—"

"I've tried that, I've tried everything," he says. "I tried talking to my parents. I tried going to a counselor. They even tried me on medication, and none of it worked. You know?"

Yes, I want to say, but don't. Not that I have personal experience with it, but. Yes. I know.

"It was just an idea," I say. "So go ahead. I'm listening."

Listening is not something I do well, but I'm going to try.

Maybe it will help.

Me, not Andy.

"Okay, so. Where do I start?"

"Kayla," I say.

Andy hesitates. "You remembered her name."

"Well—sure."

"Okay. That's impressive. I'll take that. Here we go. I met her at—"

Jack barrels through my door. "Time's up!"

I almost shriek in surprise, and Jack looks like that's exactly the reaction he was looking for. Smirking, he scoops up his laptop and hustles out of my room and down the hall.

Fine. Whatever. I kick the door shut, hoping it didn't wake up my parents.

"Sorry," I say to Andy. "Small interruption. I'm back."

"You sure?"

"Totally sure," I say, peeking through my blinds. "So tell me about your girlfriend."

"Well, she's not my girlfriend anymore, for one thing."

"Okay, so tell me about your ex-girlfriend."

"She's not my ex, either," Andy says.

"Okay, so, what is she?"

"She's dead."

Kevin Cooper wrote on your timeline.
September 2, one year ago.

Hey Tori. You want to hang out sometime after school?

Like · Comment · Share

Tori Hershberger I'm pretty busy with softball and everything.

Kevin Cooper K

NINE

"Oh . . . ," I say.

"She was killed, and there was nothing I could do," Andy says.

"Andy, I'm sorry."

"*Are* you?"

His voice turns abruptly ragged and sharp, the serrated edge of a hunting knife. Why does it seem like everyone keeps asking me that?

"Well, yeah, I mean . . . it's tragic."

Andy hesitates, then just says, "Yeah."

"We don't have to talk about this," I say.

"No, no," Andy says. "We got this far. You want to know why I'm ready to put the pedal to the metal, right?"

"Well . . ."

"That involves Kayla, and what happened to her," Andy says. "Unless you can't take it."

I shut my eyes and rub them hard until green spots dance behind my lids.

"I can take it," I say. "So . . . where'd you meet her?"

"Comic book shop. I got a job working there over the summer. It was pretty cool."

I'm glad he can't see me roll my eyes. Maybe he's not the semi-debonair guy I'd envisioned. Hot guys generally don't hang out at comic book shops, except maybe Noah, and he's only hot by comparison. He goes to one for his weirdo anime fix.

"You think I'm a big nerd now?" Andy asks, like he can read my mind.

"No," I say. But think, *Yeah, kinda.* Not the first one I've met. Or lived with.

I check my blinds again and catch Noah coming up the sidewalk. Thank God. I raise the blinds and slide open my window. By the time he gets there, I'm fumbling with the screen.

"Well, she'd just seen the newest Superman movie," Andy is saying. "That happens a lot. People see a superhero movie and then suddenly we get flooded with customers. It's probably why the industry is still alive. But she came in asking about it, and we got to talking, and one thing led to another."

"So you just took her right then and there," I manage to say while Noah helps me with the screen. After another moment we've got it, and he's climbing carefully into my room.

Thank you! I mouth.

Andy laughs. Or what amounts to a laugh for him. "No. That part was . . . different."

"Different how?" I say as Noah slides my window shut and sits on my bed. His eyebrows are squeezed together as he watches me, clearly trying to catch up to the conversation.

"I don't know, exactly," Andy says. "Do you remember your first kiss?"

My gut clenches. I look at Noah. What awful, stupid timing.

Noah mouths at me, *Put it on speaker.*

I wince and shake my head.

Noah points to himself with both hands and mouths, *Then why am I here?*

"Tori?" Andy says.

"Huh? Yeah?"

"Do you remember your first kiss?"

"Um . . . I'm going to put you on speaker, okay?" I say. "My hand's cramping up and my ear's all sweaty."

"Oh. Sure, yeah."

"Thanks."

Because I'm an idiot, I put my finger to my lips. Noah gives me a pitying look that says *No shit, Hershy.* Then I set the phone down in the middle of my mattress and tap the speaker button.

"You there?" I say.

"Loud and clear," Andy says. "Now quit stalling. Yes or no, do you remember your first kiss?"

Noah looks confused. I wave it off. "Sure," I say.

"What was it like?"

I shrug, as if Andy can see me, and start wandering around my room so I don't have to look at Noah. I can feel him following me with his eyes. "You know. Okay."

"Do you remember his name?"

As clear as the first time I struck someone out, I think.

"Uh-huh," I say.

"Well?"

"Well, it's not something I want to really talk about."

"Oh, come on. How hot and sexy can a first kiss be?"

"It's not that," I say. "It's just, the other guys put him up to it. So I felt kind of used, to be honest. If you *can* be used in seventh grade."

"Oh. Sorry, I shouldn't have pushed."

I sigh, and don't bother making it silent. I want him to hear it. "It's okay. What about yours?"

"With Kayla?"

"Or whoever."

"Kayla . . ." Andy trails off. I imagine him staring into the distance through the rainy windshield.

"It took a long time," he says finally. "To kiss, I mean."

"That's a bummer."

Noah makes a scribbling motion with his right hand. I point to my desk. He gets up, rummages around, and finds a notepad and Sharpie. On the pad he writes, "This is suicidal?"

I hold up a finger to indicate *Just wait.*

"It was okay, though," Andy is saying. "She was really . . . you know, affectionate? And I liked that. We went pretty slow. And I didn't know until then that that's kind of what I wanted."

"Are you sure you're a boy? Because the guys I know are not into slow going."

Noah offers me a big jokey shrug as if to say, *We can't help it.*

Andy gives another low laugh. "Pretty sure," he says.

"So—I mean, not to be crude or anything, but did she cheat on you or something?" That seemed to be the way these things went. So I'd heard.

Andy is silent again for a bit before saying, "No. But nobody knew. Nobody knew we were together. Everyone just thought we were friends. Really good friends, but nothing else. Even her mom didn't know. *Still* doesn't know we were together, really."

"Why didn't Kayla tell anyone you were together? Was she . . . embarrassed by you or something?" I ask. Suddenly I wonder if Andy is this disfigured monster or something, that my long-hair, high-cheekbones imagining of him is merely wishful thinking. Comic book nerd notwithstanding.

"I don't think so, not specifically. But . . . maybe. Yeah. I didn't blame her. It was kind of a first for both of us. I mean, we had to make it up as we went along."

"You never dated anyone before?"

"No one like Kayla."

I sit on the bed, beside but not too near Noah. He's leaning over with his elbows on his knees, face tight in concentration.

"What was it about her?" I ask. "What made her so special?"

"She . . . she *completed* me," Andy says.

Noah's serious face breaks, and he makes a jerk-off gesture. I almost laugh out loud, and smack his shoulder. It's such a relief having him here, but I also need him to understand just how much of my ass is on the line. He grabs the notepad again and scrawls, "Not buying it!"

I write a question mark. He writes, "This kid is not going to kill himself."

"God, I know how awful that sounds," Andy says. "It's so cliché and lame, but I don't know how else to put it. I could be who I am without worrying about it for the first time in my life, when I was with her."

He pauses.

"She made it okay to be me."

Some smart-ass remark whistles through my brain, but it's gone before I can really seize it. Then I'm grateful it's gone. I don't want to make fun of something like that. Even Noah lets that one go.

"Then my dad started getting suspicious," Andy goes on.

"Suspicious about what?"

"That we were doing a lot more than staying up all night watching movies or whatever," Andy says. "Which is exactly what we *were* doing."

"And makin' out," I can't help but say.

"Sometimes."

"He didn't like her?"

"At first he did," Andy says. "Dad thought she was cool. I mean, she was smart. Knew how to have a conversation, once she opened up a little."

Staring into the mirror over my dresser, I ask, "Was she pretty?"

I must've really hit a nerve there, because Andy is quiet for a long time. During the silence I notice Noah looking at my reflection too, from behind me. The look on his face is . . . weird.

"I wouldn't say pretty," Andy says at last. "I wouldn't *not* say it, but it's the wrong word. It was something else. She was attractive. I know that's a colossally lame kind of word, but I can't think of another one. When Kayla first came into the store, it was like . . . I don't know. . . ."

"Love at first sight?"

Noah is still looking at me in the mirror. Which, I guess, means I'm still looking at him. For a second I imagine Lucas sitting there instead. Lucas has this swagger that, to be honest, isn't unique unto itself around the upperclassman guys, especially the athletes, but his is elegant. Like he's not trying. And, sure, he comes off a little cocky, I suppose. But in a charming way. And holy crap, his *arms*, and . . .

. . . and he's not the one sitting here in my room past two in the morning when I needed someone. Even if I could have called him, he wouldn't be here. I know it. I know it like I know the bags on our infield and how second has a black mark along one corner. I just know it.

"No," Andy says, and it comes out sharp, stabbing me back

to reality. "Love at first sight is too simple. Too *neat*. It was something else. The way she carried herself. Kept her head tilted down a little. Things like that."

I break my reflected gaze from Noah's. "Oh. That's sweet."

"Yeah. It kind of was."

"So your dad found out you were hooking up . . ."

"And said he didn't approve. Neither did Mom. They thought we'd get into trouble."

"Like, pregnant?"

Andy and Noah both snort at the same time. Fortunately, Andy doesn't hear him.

"Something like that," Andy says. "They didn't actively hate her or anything, they just thought . . . maybe we weren't a good match. And then school started getting tough on her. . . ."

Noah leans closer to the phone. I nod and point to it, as if to say, *See? Here it comes.* I could hear it in Andy's voice.

When he speaks again, his voice is tighter, like his throat has started to close up on him.

"She was catching a lot of shit," Andy says. "She was never real popular, you know, just didn't make a lot of friends or anything. That never bothered me. But I went to a different school. There wasn't much I could do to help."

Noah hits the mute button.

"I'm still not buying it," he says, keeping his voice low.

I hunch my shoulders, feeling profoundly guilty for saying, "Yeah . . . me either. I mean, I *am* pretty sure he's serious about—you know, going through with it, but not . . .”

"Not because of her. His girlfriend.”

"Right! Or . . . maybe he just hasn't gotten to the real reason yet, I don't know.”

"See if you can get him to go there,” Noah says. "Figure out what's really going on.”

"See if you can get me to go where, exactly?”

I suck in a breath. Noah's eyes bug out.

"So, Tori,” Andy says, as if the rage in his voice is held back only by tightly clamped teeth. "Wanna tell me who your friend is?”

Kevin Cooper wrote on your timeline.
September 21, one year ago.

You got that same backpack. my smiley is still
on the strap. :)

Like · Comment · Share

Tori Hershberger Yep.

TEN

"Well?" Andy says.

"Uh . . . hi?" Noah says, and his voice breaks. Normally, I'd laugh. Not now.

"Who the fuck is this?" Andy demands.

"My name's Noah," Noah says. "I'm friends with—"

"Oh, *Noah*, of course," Andy says. "I should've guessed. So nice to meet you, *Noah*. So how long you been joining us there in the studio audience, *Noah*?"

"I just got here, man, I swear."

"I don't believe you."

"He doesn't live very far," I say quickly. "Andy, just hold on a second, please?"

"Why?" Andy spits. "So you can bullshit me into saying something else I only meant for you to hear?"

"It's not like that!" I say. "I'm scared for you, okay? And I'm scared for me, and I needed help, so I called Noah. I wasn't trying to piss you off or make a fool out of you or anything. Come on, please? You can trust Noah, I swear."

Noah and I both stare at the crappy little flip phone like it's a video screen instead, as if we can see Andy's reaction if we just stare hard enough.

My ribs constrict when I hear the engine rev. My hand jets out and grabs Noah's, all on its own. Noah squeezes my hand in return.

After a minute Andy says, "So what'd she tell you so far, Noah old buddy, old chum?"

Noah clears his throat. "Well . . . that you're having a tough time, that you called this number at random . . . and that you're pretty serious about killing yourself."

"Ding-ding, you win," Andy says, his voice dry. "And now explain why I shouldn't just roll on down this road and off the side of a cliff, considering my entire point has been that the whole world screws each other over, and that's clearly true here as well?"

"That's not what I meant," I say before Noah can answer. "You're not being fair."

"Yeah? Lotta that going around," Andy replies. "How could you do this, Tori?"

"You can trust him," I repeat.

"Like I trusted you?"

And for whatever reason, maybe because it's so late and I'm so tired-not-tired, or maybe because the past couple of months have been such a royal bitch . . . I slide to the floor on my knees, so that my body rests on top of my mattress. I pull the phone close.

"Andy?" I say. "Please. I want to help. I'll listen. We both will. I just want the sun to come up and for you to be okay and for all this to be in the past, okay? I'm sorry I didn't tell you Noah was here, but I needed help. I couldn't do this by myself anymore."

Noah, who hasn't let go of my hand, squeezes it again.

"Andy, just please don't do something that you can't take back," I say. "All right?"

"Do you want me to go?" Noah asks. "Because I will, no problem. I wasn't trying to mess with you, man. I swear. I'm just here for Tori. We go way back."

Andy snorts. "Like I could know you really left even if I told you to."

"For what it's worth," Noah says, and his face is un-Noah-like serious, "I wouldn't do that to you. If you want me to go, I will go."

"What, is that supposed to be your word of honor?"

Noah shakes his head, then blinks as he realizes he's done it and Andy can't see it. I know the feeling. Funny how our body language doesn't change over the phone.

"No," Noah says. "The samurai never gave their word. They just said what they would do and it got done."

"So you're like a ninja now or something?"

"No. Samurai were totally different."

"Hey, Tori?"

"Yeah," I say. "I'm here."

"Is this guy as big a dork as he sounds?"

I feel a minuscule smile tug my lips. "Bigger," I say.

Noah gives me a smile about the same size as my own.

"Yeah?" Andy says. "So you crushing on him, too?"

I can't answer. And the fact that I can't throws me completely off. *No,* I want to say. *No, of course not, he's Noah. If you knew him and you knew me, you'd understand we could never—*

"We're just friends," Noah says, then seems to suddenly notice he's got my hand. He carefully pulls it away from mine. "Really good friends."

"Uh-huh," Andy says. "Well, isn't that nice. Nice to have friends like that. People you can count on. Huh, Tori?"

"Yes," I whisper. The skin on my hand cools where Noah had held it.

"What's that? I couldn't hear you."

"Yes," I say, louder. "It's nice. It's good." Weak, but it's all I can manage.

Andy doesn't reply right away. I stare emptily at the phone, trying to ignore Noah's expression in my periphery. I don't want to know what he's thinking. I don't know why I don't want to know.

I guess I don't know much of *anything.*

"Okay," Andy says at last. "I'll see this part through, anyway."

"What part?" Noah asks, and I'm grateful because I can't seem to make myself ask the question.

"About the love of my life," Andy says. "So where was

I? I mean, now that there's a crowd, I guess I should dance, right?"

Noah and I both sink a little, like in relief. We're back on track. No idea where we're headed, but at least I'm not alone.

"You were talking about Kay . . ." Noah hesitates. "Kaylynn?"

"Kayla," Andy and I say in unison.

"Right," Andy goes on. "School. Those assholes. They just wouldn't leave her alone, you know? Kept pushing and pushing. . . ."

"What do you mean, 'pushing'?" Noah asks.

I think I know, but there's no way I'm going to pipe up and say it.

"Making fun of her," Andy says. "How she looked, how she dressed, how she talked. Everything. And then a few weeks ago she was driving over to my place, so we could hang out, you know, and . . . just got real emotional . . . and . . ."

Noah and I sit absolutely still. Before he even says it, I know where Andy's going with this. Not a doubt in my mind now.

"I guess she didn't see the turn," Andy says quietly. "Or maybe I just hope she didn't."

I honestly can't tell if he's crying or not. I honestly can't tell if I am either. I don't, usually. Not often. It's just not my way of dealing. But the pattern on my bedspread does seem to blur a little.

"Just sailed right off," Andy continues in the same soft voice. "Probably didn't feel anything, anyway. One quick snap. Or crash. And done."

That's why he is where he is tonight. Just like I thought. In his mind, there's a poetry to it. Drama. Just like this phone call.

He *is* serious, and he wants it just so.

"Was that here?" I ask him, lowering my voice to match his.

"Huh?"

"Was that in town?" I say.

"You mean, in Canyon? Yeah . . . I mean, not in town, it was just outside of town. Up here, in the mountains. Yeah. Why?"

"I just didn't hear about it," I say.

"Yeah, because you're so tuned in to the news," Noah says.

I give him a look.

"It *did* make the news," Andy says. "But so what? Reporting it didn't bring her back. Reporting it didn't make those ass-holes change their minds about her."

"Well, that's what makes them assholes," Noah says.

Andy snorts a laugh.

"What did you want them to do?" I hear myself saying. I'm looking at Noah when I do it.

"Who?" Andy says.

"The assholes," I say.

Noah meets my gaze. It takes all of a millisecond for him to see that I'm talking to *him* just as much as to Andy. Because when Noah says "assholes," I know he's talking about Lucas and them.

"What did you *want* them to do?" I go on, still eyeing Noah. "What could they have done afterward to make you not be where you are tonight?"

Noah frowns at me. Andy is silent.

"I mean, no offense," I say, as anger starts burning my face. "But lots of people's lives suck, and they don't commit suicide. It's not someone else's fault, it's their own. Right? Isn't it? Are you trying to say that if you drive off a cliff tonight, that's on *me*? . . . Because, you know what? My calendar's full. This is not my problem. Too many people have already made their lives my problem, and it's not fair, okay?"

I have to stop and catch my breath. After a second of silence it slowly filters through what I've said. How it must sound. I scramble my brain backward, trying to figure a way to back-track my way out of it.

Andy does the job for me.

"Noah?" he says.

"Uh—yeah," Noah goes.

"Why is she talking like that?"

Noah raises his eyebrows to me.

"Because," Andy says, coughing a bit, "Victoria, dear, I gotta tell ya, that was not overly helpful right now. So how about we tally up which of us has had the most bullshit to put up with and see who wins, huh? Let's go, you wise fucking sage of the universe."

Andy laughs, and it's forced, and it grates, and I have to close my eyes against it. My God, how could I be so stupid? I should've kept my mouth shut.

"See, I knew I shouldn't have trusted you," Andy goes on. "I knew I shouldn't trust anyone anymore. I never should have picked up the phone in the first place. *God*, I'm so fuck-ing stupid!"

His echo of my own thoughts snaps me back. "Andy, come on, I'm sor—"

"No!" he barks. "This is exactly what I've been trying to tell you all night. People are all the same. They just dump on you, over and over and over again. Even when they see what it's doing to you, they keep it up. And I've had it. *That's* why I'm up here tonight, all right? So maybe me losing the love of my life isn't a big deal in your world, fine. Maybe in the vast cosmic ocean of life, it's not even a heartbeat. But it was the *end*, Tori. Is that penetrating your tiny wee skull even one millimeter? This camel's breaking his own back before the last straw does."

"Andy—"

"I mean, who are you to sit there and judge what I'm going through? Huh? What's so god-awful in your life that gives you the right to tell me mine doesn't suck? Let's go. I call. Play your cards."

My eyes lose focus. It's not from lack of sleep, although that's becoming an issue. This is that stare-into-middle-space thing, that little ministroke you get sometimes, even when you can hear and sense everything that's going on around you.

On reflex, I clear my throat.

"Nothing," I say, and my voice is way, way too steady. "Nothing much. I only killed a guy, so . . . you win, I guess."

Kevin Cooper wrote on your timeline.
October 21.

did you see my car this morning? do you know
who did it?

Like · Comment · Share

Tori Hershberger What are you talking about?

Kevin Cooper Seriously Tori do you know???
bcause I am going to kick their fucking asses!!!

Tori Hershberger Take it easy. It was just a
joke.

Kevin Cooper HAHAHA. fag queerbag, assfucker,
yeh soooo funny and its not coming off either. they
ruined my fucking car!! my mom had to see it tori.

Tori Hershberger I'm sure it'll come off. They
were just messing around.

Kevin Cooper why are you being like this?
that's not fair tori. I need this like I need a thumb
up my ass.

👍 Marly DeSoto likes this.

Tori Hershberger Marlycat! Why would you like
that?!

Marly DeSoto I was giving him a thumb.

👍 You and six others like this.

Albert Jiminez BAM!

Dakota Lorey BAM!

Lucas Mulcahy BAM BAM!

Kevin Cooper Fuck you all. thanks, tori. way to go CHAMP.

Tori Hershberger Look, it was just a joke, I promise. They didn't mean anything. I'll clean up your car, I swear.

Kevin Cooper So you knew they were going to do it

Tori Hershberger No! Just stop for a minute, okay? I'll take care of it.

ELEVEN

"Wait, what?" Andy says after a long pause.

Noah shuts his eyes.

"Listen, I'm gonna need coffee, PFQ," I say, rubbing my face and standing up.

Noah says, "Tori . . ."

"I'm not kidding," I say. "Andy, I'm still here, I'm still talking to you, or listening, or whatever, but it's—"

I look at my alarm clock. Feel my shoulders drop.

"—almost three in the morning," I say. "If I don't get some caffeine in me, things are going to get ugly. Know what I'm saying?"

"Um—okay," Andy says quietly.

"Good. Now, I have to go into my kitchen to make the coffee. Noah will be happy to keep you busy, right, Noah?"

"Um. Sure. Yeah," Noah says.

"Super," I say. "Be back in a minute."

I open my door and walk quietly down the hall, grateful it's carpeted. Mom and Dad's bedroom is dark. Dim light peeps out from under Jack's door, but I don't hear anything in his room.

There's a hanging light fixture over the breakfast bar that separates the living room from the kitchen. Mom's very big on "open space." It's plenty of light to see by. I open the percolator and find Jack's grounds virtually dry in the filter, so I plug the machine back in and it burbles to life. Everything's going great until my elbow smacks into the key ring hanging against the wall and knocks Jack's keys to the tile floor with a clatter the size of our school marching band.

I sit on one of the tall breakfast bar stools and use both hands to rub my eyes, then my head. *So* tired. And yet I somehow instinctively know when I go back into my room, Andy will be wide awake. Perky, even. Which is strange, if you think about it. Shouldn't he be exhausted too? Unless he's getting some kind of weird energy jolt from all this. Maybe his adrenaline is pumping. If it is, that can only be because he's really still thinking about driving that Sentra right into oblivion.

Just like Kevin.

Oblivion.

They almost rhyme.

Shouldn't have closed my eyes and thought of Kevin. I can still see the messages, just as clear as when the DA displayed them on a projector during the hearing that proved, apparently, that we deserve to be charged with everything in the law books except first-degree murder. I'm sure Allison Summers would've loved for that to have happened.

When is this going to end? Or maybe when isn't as important as *how*. . . .

Conversation started October 29.

Tori Hershberger Are you okay? I heard about the fight. Did you really get kicked out?

Kevin Cooper No I got ISS. Probably out of pity. I didn't exactly kick his ass.

Tori Hershberger What did Lucas do to you?

Kevin Cooper I took a fist on the left cheek and a foot in the ribs. I'm okay.

Tori Hershberger No, I mean, what did he ever do *to* you? Why did you pick a fight with him?

Kevin Cooper I DIDN'T!! he just wouldnt shut up. I tried to ignore him and Mr. Black was late to class and he just kept pushing Tori. so I lost it I blew up and I decked him and tried to throw a desk at him. I did not pick a fight with him

Tori Hershberger Okay. Sorry.

Kevin Cooper Rachel broke up with me.

Tori Hershberger What happened?

Kevin Cooper I cheated on her. Basically.

Tori Hershberger Cooper! You scallywag! With who?

Kevin Cooper Different school, doesn't matter. She'll be happier this way anyway.

Tori Hershberger Wow. That was like a record. Two years or something, right?

Kevin Cooper Yeah.

Kevin Cooper Thanks for listening Tori. This would have been a lot easier to text. do you still even have my number?

Kevin Cooper Hello? Hershy? You there?

TWELVE

"WHUH?!"

I bolt upright and swing my arms in a wide arc before sliding off the stool and ending up on my ass on the kitchen tile.

Oh shit, I fell asleep.

Oh shit, Andy.

Oh shit.

I stumble to my room, "Andy?" I say to Noah, who is sitting on my bed, back against the wall, ankles crossed. My phone is still face-up on the mattress.

"Uh-huh," Andy says over the phone. "Thought I lost you for a while there. Get your coffee?"

I blink, blink again, blink some more.

"What did you . . . ?" I say to Noah.

"Nothing," Noah says. "I told him about the Tokugawa Dynasty."

"It was fascinating," Andy deadpans.

"I'll bet," I say. I rub my eyes, which burn. "Lemme grab my coffee. Sorry."

I double back to the kitchen. The coffee's done. I look at the clock, shaped like a cow, hanging over the kitchen door. Mom insists it's "quirky." It's close to four a.m.

I pour a healthy splash of Coffee-mate into a mug before filling it the rest of the way with coffee. Then I head back to my room, closing the door behind me.

"Sorry it took so long," I say.

"No problem," Andy says. "You're a good friend."

I give Noah a suspicious look. "What makes you say that?"

"You came back, didn't you?" Andy says. "You didn't leave me hanging."

You know how in movies there's a smash cut that lasts just a frame or two of some weird flashback? I get one of those. Of Kevin.

. . . didn't leave me hanging . . .

I shake my head and slurp a quick gulp of coffee, and don't say anything in response. I sit at my desk, which is empty now except for a couple of books and papers. I should probably clean up the dust pattern left behind by my laptop. Someday.

Mom and Dad took the computer away the day I got arrested. Until that afternoon, I think they thought the same thing I did: that it would all blow over. Feeling the cold steel of handcuffs slapped around my wrists gave things a certain, shall we say, clarity. The prosecutor meant business. And he meant it *hard*. That was the night I scrolled through the newspaper comments online. Not a good day.

"You want me to remind you where we were?" Andy says.

I take another sip of coffee, and realize it is surprisingly perfectly made. I always misjudge how much creamer to use, but not this time. The coffee is like liquid fire from the gods. I literally sigh after the first swallow, like in a commercial.

"No," I say. "I remember. I just can't tell you."

"What? Why?"

"My lawyer said not to talk about it."

"Lawyer," Andy goes. "Holy crap. You're not kidding around. Are you?"

"Hey, I promised I'd stop asking you that, now you promise me, okay?"

"So you really did kill someone?"

"*No!*"

I grit my teeth and pause, waiting to see if Mom and Dad's door opens. I don't hear anything. Noah crosses his arms.

"No," I repeat, quietly. "He . . . killed himself. I didn't have anything to do with it. None of us did. But the district attorney says we did, so now we're gearing up for a big court fight."

"You mean a trial."

"Yes, a trial, all right?"

"You're on trial for murder."

Andy is really good at stating questions as facts. It's becoming an irritant.

"Basically," I say. It's not the kind of statement *or* question that gets easier to hear or speak over time.

"So this guy committed suicide?" Andy asks.

"Yeah."

"Well, I guess that explains our initial awkwardness," Andy says quietly. Then, in a normal voice, he says, "How'd he do it?"

"Hung himself," I say, as the coffee begins congealing in my throat. "With a belt or scarf or something."

"Hanged."

"Yeah."

"No, I mean, the word is 'hanged.' When it refers to a person, it's always 'hanged,' not 'hung.' It's grammatically correct, although I truly do not know why."

My eyelids freeze in place, wide open. "Are you seriously giving me a grammar lesson right now?"

"Just saying," Andy goes. And for whatever reason, probably because I'm so damn tired, I hear-feel that weird cellphone-on-a-wooden-table *reeee* in my head again.

"So what was his name?" Andy asks.

I take a drink of my coffee. Mr. Halpern specifically said not to do this. Talk, I mean, not drink coffee.

"Kevin Cooper," I say.

"That's been on the news," Andy says slowly.

"Yeah."

"You're one of the Canyon City Seven."

Can I just take a time-out at this point to say how stupid that term is? I don't want to say so to Andy, because—well, just *because*—but I mean, come on. We don't deserve a big media label like that, like we were burning crosses or going around as a gang and curb-stomping kittens or something. That isn't what happened, not at all.

"Technically, I am, yes, but listen, you can't believe all that stuff they're saying," I tell Andy. Talking about this again brings me to my feet. I start pacing. Bed, closet, bed, closet. I'm magically not tired anymore. Or maybe it's the coffee. Noah watches me but keeps his mouth shut.

"Why should I not believe it?" Andy asks. "What say you, Noah? Who should I believe?"

"I think this one is between you two," Noah says.

I jump in. "Why should you not believe it? Because it's bullshit, that's why not! Jesus!"

"Okay, okay," Andy says. "Just asking. What really happened then? What did you do?"

"I didn't do anything, that's what I'm saying. Look, I'm not even supposed to talk about this. I can't. It's a legal thing."

Andy sighs. He doesn't speak for a few seconds.

"My life is in your hands, Tori," he says finally. "Maybe you should talk about anything I *want* you to talk about."

My jaw falls open so hard I hear something in my right ear pop. Noah, too, looks down at the phone, his eyebrows mashing together.

"Wait a sec, are you, like, blackmailing me with your own life?"

"I guess. Yeah."

"Dude," Noah says.

"You realize how messed up that is, right?" I say.

"I was messed up long before I called you, so, whatever."

"Hold on. It's one thing to say you're going to kill yourself because your girlfriend died. It's entirely another thing to say you'll do it if I don't make some big confession to you."

Andy snorts. "Hey, I'm the loco one here. And it's not *just* because the person I loved most in the world died. It's how people *feel* about it that's got me up here. It's not pain, Tori. It's hopelessness."

I look to Noah. He shakes his head and shrugs like he's not sure whether to believe Andy or not.

I mouth the words, *I can't risk it.*

Noah frowns again, then nods. Then he wiggles his thumb in the air and mouths, *Mute.*

I tap the mute button, double and triple checking that it's on this time. "Andy?" I say, just to check.

There's no response. Noah and I speak quickly.

"I have to keep talking," I say, whispering even though there's no reason to. I can't risk him using any excuse to drive off that cliff. "Maybe he's not serious—or not anymore, anyway—but I can't afford that chance."

"No, I get it," Noah says. "He's not sounding good. He sounds like . . . like he just doesn't give a crap anymore. That can't be good."

"No." I rub my eyes again. They feel as dry and leathery as my mitt.

"You'd better tell him," Noah says gently, like he knows it won't be easy.

And it won't. Going over the whole story again . . . dammit, why did he have to call *this* number? My number is on his phone, and the chances it would be destroyed in a car wreck, even a bad one, are pretty small unless the Sentra explodes, like he talked about, but I think he's right that it wouldn't really happen. . . .

. . . And I can't believe I am even *thinking* about it. I mean, my God! How can I be standing here considering the "legal ramifications" of my cell number being on the phone of another dead kid? Am I that self-involved?

No. It's not that; it can't be that. This is a perfectly legit and reasonable fear.

Isn't it? I mean, I'm in enough trouble as it is, that's all, so I just have to be cautious.

That's all.

Andy's voice smacks me back to the phone. "So tell me about it. What did you do?"

Since he's sort of backed me into a corner, I take a breath. My eyes close. I have this part memorized. Seared, really, into my head, where I'm sure it will stay for the rest of my life.

I hit the mute button.

"Aggravated manslaughter," I say, and hope he can't hear the way my voice shakes.

"Um, okay," Andy says, "can you say it again except this time pretend I haven't actually graduated from law school?"

"It just means that I said some things that weren't real nice, and he killed himself over it, and now they're blaming me," I say, practically choking on the words. "*Us*, I mean. Blaming us."

"Well, what did you say?" Andy asks.

"Nothing! I mean . . . nothing worse than what everyone else said." I run a hand through my hair, pick up my coffee, put it down again. Not so thirsty anymore, it turns out.

"So that makes it okay."

There he goes with that statement-question thing again.

"I didn't say that," I tell him.

"Okay, back up for a minute," Andy says. "How exactly did you know Kevin? Cooper, was it?"

I slump to my bed. But even if I did lie down, I wouldn't sleep now. Absurdly, I wish Noah would put his arm around me, even if just for a few minutes.

"Kevin was a friend of mine," I say.

"*Oh*," Andy says, sounding surprised. Noah frowns a bit.

"Not a good friend," I add, and feel a quick needle prick of guilt in my stomach. I'm not lying; Kevin Cooper was never my best friend, or even a good friend.

But a friend? Yes. I can admit it to myself even if I'm not supposed to to anyone else, according to Mr. Halpern.

"Just someone I knew," I say to Andy. "From around. You know. My mom calls it a perfect storm."

I close my eyes and rub them with my fingers. I don't bother to tell Andy that I think she's right. I also don't tell him that we used to be better friends in junior high. Even last year, a little. Things changed this year, that's all. It happens all the time. Softball was going really well; I was making new friends, even with the upperclassmen like Marly and Lucas and everyone. Things just—changed.

Andy says, "Hmph," and that's all.

"The county attorney has a thing about being hard on juvenile crime, or whatever," Noah adds, looking at me as if for permission.

"Yeah," I agree. "I guess that's me. And the others. Juvenile criminals. And um . . ."

I pause, because this isn't getting any easier to talk about.

"So his mom found the Facebook stuff, and printed it out and made copies and everything, and took it to the cops. They investigated everything and took it to the county attorney, who probably would have, like, given us misdemeanors at most."

"Would have?" Andy repeats.

"The *New Times* got ahold of it," I say. "I assume from Kevin's mom, but I don't know. And it turns out this one kid, named Paul I think, he's thirteen . . . he shot at some horses with a BB gun, and they charged him with some kind of cruelty to animals crime. . . ."

"Wait, hold up, what's that got to do with Facebook?" Andy asks.

"Oh, I'm getting there. So they charge this kid Paul with felony cruelty to animals. This was just over the summer. So this bitch of a writer for the *New Times*, Allison Summers, goes all ballistic about it. You know, 'This kid was charged with a

felony, but kids older than him who,' um . . ." I clear my throat.
"'Who allegedly talked this poor gay kid into committing suicide, they get off with nothing.' And I guess a lot of people read
the *New Times*, because the next thing I know, we're getting
charged with stuff like aggravated manslaughter and . . . and
now they're calling it a hate crime, so if we get found guilty,
that could add like ten years to any sentence, and . . ."

And that's as far as I can go.

I press my lips together and hold them shut with my free
hand. Jesus, what am I going to do?

"Why are you telling me all this?" Andy says.

I blurt out a gasp. "Because you *asked*!"

"Nah, no," Andy says, and I can imagine him shaking
his head, long hair waving. If he has long hair, I mean. "You
didn't actually have to tell me all that. You could've made
up anything you wanted. But instead you told me the whole
story. How come?"

He's got a point.

"I don't know," I say.

"Sure you do," Andy says. "I mean, this is really serious."

"It's really *bullshit*."

Andy doesn't reply. I don't add anything. We sit there for a
minute. Noah cracks his knuckles one at a time. For no good
reason, it occurs to me that he hasn't yawned once tonight.

"Okay," Andy says finally. "Why is it bullshit?"

And it all comes out. Like soda from a shaken bottle, bub-
bling, frothing, and pissing you off as you try to get out of its way.

"Okay, for one thing? He wasn't gay! He had a girlfriend for like two years. Rachel. So what the hell is up with this hate crime shit, you know? That's totally not fair! What if I called a white guy the n-word and then shot him in the face? Is that a hate crime? No!"

"I'd think the shooting-him-in-the-face part is a hate crime," Andy says.

"I didn't do anything wrong!" I shout, ignoring both Andy's comment and how late—or early—it is. "It was a bunch of stupid jokes on stupid Facebook, for God's sake. Happens to everyone, all the time, what makes him so special?"

"He's dead."

My emotional explosion ends. I'm left holding a simile of a sticky bottle of flat soda.

"That's not my fault," I say.

"I didn't say it was," Andy goes. "Just that—you know, you asked why he's different, and that's what's different. That's all."

"But you see what I'm saying, right?" I demand. I didn't realize until just now how badly I need someone to take my side. Not just out of loyalty, like Noah, or family, like Mom. Someone who really does see my side of the story. "I didn't *kill* him. I wasn't there, I didn't throw him off the balcony."

"No," Andy says. "I suppose you didn't."

"What?" I say, not liking the way he says it.

"Uh, *what* what?"

"You want to say something, I can hear it in your voice," I tell him. "What is it?"

"Nothing," Andy says. "I don't know. Go on."

I rub my eyes again. "That's it, that's all there is."

"Are you sure?"

I try to keep it in. It comes out anyway.

"People think I'm this homophobic murderer!" I shout, again oblivious to how I'm almost certainly going to wake up Mom or Dad any second now. "And now they're saying shit about me, like I'm this terrible person, and I'm not! That's why I don't have a computer, I'm not stupid, I know why they took it!"

I probably am making no sense to Andy now, probably not even to Noah, who knows most of this already, and I don't care. It feels good to get all this out.

"They just don't want me to see what people are saying about me! I saw some of it before they took my laptop, and holy crap, you want to talk about 'mean girls'? You want to talk about saying hateful things online? You wouldn't believe the stuff people are saying. About all of us. Someone even threw a brick through my mom's car window. A *brick*! Isn't that assault? How about attempted murder, why isn't anyone being charged with *that*, huh?"

"So it's a cycle," Andy says, and his voice is maddeningly calm. I want him to get angry with me. *For* me.

"Yeah," I say, finally feeling a little spent, and sitting on my bed. "Something like that."

"People are bullying you for being a bully," Andy goes on.

"I'm not a *bully*. I told you it was just jokes."

"Well, but why were you making fun of him, then? I mean, why make the jokes at all?"

"Because I thought he . . ."

I bite my lip. This part hasn't exactly been brought up yet.

"Thought he, what? Was gay?"

"He wasn't," I repeat. "No, it's not that. I know he wasn't."

"Okay, so you thought he—what?"

"I thought he knew I was kidding," I say. And several of the words crack like an old bat.

"Oh yeah?" Andy says. "How do you figure?"

"I told you he was kind of a friend of mine," I say, and feel like it's a confession that's been beaten out of me. "That first kiss we talked about? Yeah, well. Mine was Kevin."

Tori Hershberger We are taking State this year. That's right. I said it.

Like · Comment · Share · November 15

👍3 people like this.

Marly DeSoto go tori! its your birthday! go tori!

👍You and 2 others like this.

Lucas Mulcahy is it your birthday tori????

👍You like this.

Marly DeSoto lucas you're so dumb. its an old joke.

👍2 people like this.

Albert Jiminez Lucas was just a kid when people were saying that. He doesn't know.

👍You and 2 others like this.

Tori Hershberger Thanks Marlycat! :) Lucas, don't listen to Albert. <3

👍You like this.

Kevin Cooper You can do it Tori!

👍You like this.

Marly DeSoto no one asked you cooper. go read Twilight again.

👍You and 3 others like this.

THIRTEEN

"Whoa," Andy says. "You kissed him?"

"Just once. But yeah."

"How?"

"Well, not with *tongue* . . ."

"Oh my *God*, no," Andy says, and Noah doesn't even try to suppress a laugh. "I mean, how did it come about?"

I feel myself blush. "Oh. Right. Well, that's the thing, the other boys put him up to it. I don't think he really wanted to do it. We were at a school dance and they kind of surrounded us and pushed him into it."

"I remember that," Noah says.

"*No*-ah," Andy sings, "did you help push him into it?"

"No," Noah says. "We didn't really know each other at the time."

"Did you wish you were the pushee?" Andy goes on.

I think it takes Noah and me the exact same number of moments to figure out Andy's phrasing. Because when I get it, I look at Noah and he looks at me at the same time.

Noah lets his mouth fall open, but it's another second or two before he answers, "I probably wouldn't have needed to be pushed, no."

Softball and baseball are slow sports for the most part. They're more about the drama, for lack of a better word: the *story*. The Yankees versus the Red Sox, or rooting for the Cubbies every year because, well, Jesus, they've got to catch a break someday, right? But sometimes there's a moment, whether it's a high school field or a major stadium, when everything changes. Bill Buckner missing an easy grounder, or a three-run homer to tie a game. It brings both the home and visiting crowds to their feet, and every speck of dust flying around the infield becomes charged with history.

Well—that's what just happened. A game changer.

Noah clearly sees it too. He almost looks apologetic, like he knows the timing couldn't be worse. Luckily—ha-ha—we have Andy to keep us occupied.

"But Kevin was pushed," Andy says. "Or cajoled, or put-upon, or . . . bullied . . ."

"Yeah," I say, before Andy can keep going. "They said he was a—"

"What?"

"Sorry. I'm just a little sensitive about word choice right now."

"All things considered, I doubt you have much to fear from me, Tori."

"Faggot. They said if he didn't kiss me, then he must be a faggot."

Noah winces. He must remember that part too.

"Ah," Andy says.

"Yeah. I wish he wouldn't have done it."

"Did you stop him?"

"Not exactly."

"Why?"

I shrug. "He was cute."

Andy snorts a laugh. Noah raises an eyebrow.

"But still," I say, "in retrospect, he shouldn't have done it if he didn't want to."

"How do you know he didn't? You sound pretty cute to me."

I let the second part of that comment slide, because I have no idea where to go with it. I avoid Noah's eyes.

"He wanted to kiss Rachel Roland, not me," I say.

"They ended up dating for two years," Noah adds.

"Right, exactly," I say. "He even apologized to me for kissing me. He said it wasn't personal. So, okay. Whatever."

"Did it bother you?" Noah asks me.

"What, that he did it?"

"That he did it but didn't want to."

"I don't—no, it didn't. Not in so many words."

"How many words does it take?"

"Look, you didn't see his face when he was coming in," I

say. "It looked like he was smelling dog poop. It was a real confidence booster. So fine, sure, maybe it did bug me."

"Uh-huh," Andy says, and I imagine instantly what he's thinking: *But you're still alive and he's not.*

This thought makes me mad. I can't help it. "He should have stuck up for himself. Why wouldn't he do that? They would have left him alone then."

"How do you figure that?" Andy says.

"Sixth grade," I say. "First day of school. New bus, new route. This Godzilla-size jerk named Vince Bretz, I'll never forget his name—"

"Oh yeah!" Noah says. "Screw that guy! Sorry."

"I know, right?" I say. "So Vince Bretz is sitting about in the middle of the bus. And every boy who walks down the aisle, he trips. And every one of them gets up and either punches Vince in the arm, or yells at him, or shoves him, and each time, Vince just laughs. But he never tripped them again either."

"Let me guess," Andy says.

Noah pinches the bridge of his nose, nodding.

"Exactly," I say. "Except for Kevin. Kevin just got up and went back the other way, sitting up front by himself. *Sixth* grade. What might've been different if he'd hit Vince too that day?"

"Well," Andy says, "I hate to state the obvious, but I guess we'll never know."

"Yeah."

"Sooo . . . I dunno, can I just . . . ? I don't want to put

words in your mouth or anything, but are you saying it's his fault?"

"Kinda. Yeah. Yeah, I am. Sorry if that makes me a bitch or whatever, but that's what happens when you let someone push you around."

"It does reveal a lot about your worldview."

"'Worldview'? I thought you said you were sixteen."

"A very precocious sixteen."

"And what's it reveal?" I almost add, *O wise sage of the universe*, just to stick it to him, let him know how it feels, but I don't.

"It reveals that you believe every human being on earth should have the innate ability to defend him or herself, and if they can't, they deserve to—"

"Hold on!" I say, partly because I don't agree with what he's about to say, and partly because I just can't hear him say it.

"What?" Andy says.

"You *are* putting words in my mouth," I say. "That's exactly what you're doing."

"No, I'm extrapolating a belief system based on what you said about Kevin."

"Well, you can stop. It's not true."

"What's not true? I haven't said anything yet. You cut me off."

I shake my head and squeeze my eyes shut. He's starting to sound like all the lawyers. I can't keep up.

"Just, whatever," I say. I turn to Noah for help. He raises his shoulders with a *What do you want me to do?* look.

"I think this is important," Andy insists. "Clearly you feel that victims are somehow to blame for their situations."

Furious, I say, "Maybe they are. How about that? Maybe they are. Kevin was. And I am too."

Andy grunts. "You're a victim? Explain that one to me."

"I told you, people are talking all kinds of shit about me! But I'm still here."

Andy doesn't respond for a minute, which is good, because it takes me that long just to settle down.

"You really believe that?" Noah asks, quietly. So quiet, I'm not sure Andy hears. If he does, he doesn't say anything.

"I don't know," I say. I take a breath, collect my thoughts. What's left of them. "Okay, no, not exactly. Maybe it's not Kevin's fault. But all I did was make one tiny joke on Facebook that wasn't even all that mean, and now it looks like my life is essentially over. So, sorry if I'm feeling a little pissy."

"You're right," Andy finally says, and I have to drag myself back to his part of the conversation.

"What?" I say.

"You're right," Andy repeats. "You're still here. Kevin gave up. I guess I never really thought about it like that."

"What do you mean, 'never'?"

"I just mean, did he ever ask for help? With like, you know . . . depression, or that he was being pushed around, anything like that?"

"Not that I know of."

"Huh." After a pause, Andy says, "What do you think your chances are? Really."

"What, you mean to get out of it? Like, not go to jail?"

"Yeah."

Noah leans forward, eyeing me carefully. My mouth goes dry.

"I don't know," I say. "Maybe pretty good, I guess. We didn't think it would even go to trial, though, so, we're kind of already screwed in one sense. Our lawyer said there's precedent in other states to be found not guilty. It's kind of a bogus bunch of charges anyway."

"How do you figure that?"

"Well, come on, it's not like I tied the rope around his neck."

"Scarf," Andy says.

"What?"

"It was a scarf, wasn't it? Not a rope."

"Yeah. Right. Sorry. Where did you . . . ?"

"In the news," Andy says. "So, now how did you get onto his Facebook page in the first place? Had he friended you?"

"Well—yeah. A while back. But it wasn't his page, it was mine."

"Yours."

"Yeah?"

"So he trusted you."

I don't reply because something black and spiny erupts in my stomach.

Tori Hershberger Whoever dreamed up high heels should be made to wear them all day at someone's wedding. My feet hurt like hell!

Like · Comment · Share · January 5

👍2 people like this.

Noah Murphy whose wedding?

Tori Hershberger I don't even know her. Some friend of my mom's.

Kevin Cooper I'm sure you were very pretty.

👍You like this.

Marly DeSoto cooper got married? so they finally legalized that in this state, huh? BAM!

👍You and 4 others like this.

Lucas Mulcahy BAM!

👍You like this.

Kevin Cooper Srsly? wtf did I ever do to you marly?

👍Noah Murphy likes this.

Lucas Mulcahy queerbag

👍5 people like this.

FOURTEEN

When the black spines in my gut shrink back a bit, I say, "He just sent messages from time to time, that's it," and feel utterly stupid for having said it. Don't I have any better defenses than these?

"Okay," Andy says, "but that last post was pretty pointed, wasn't it? From what I read."

"Maybe, but . . . well, come on! I can't read his mind. God, you and my brother, I swear."

"What about your brother?"

Noah's face acts like a physical translator to Andy's voice, making the expressions I imagine Andy is making. It would be funny if I weren't so tired.

I wonder if Andy's safe now. I wonder if I can get off the phone and finally go to sleep.

"We're not on the best of terms," I say.

"How come?" Andy says.

"Well, partly it's because we're not exactly rich, and the biggest pools of money we had saved up were for college. Me and him, my brother, I mean. We had to dive into that to pay for the lawyer."

"Oh. Suck."

"Yeah. I'll be lucky to get into one of those faux colleges they advertise on TV during the day. I had my sights set on U of A, but that's looking pretty unlikely at present."

"And your brother?"

"He's pissed. I mean, the money comes from my account first, obviously, but if it's not enough, then . . ."

The spiny black creature reappears in my gut. What the hell? I thought I was handling this all right. Maybe it's lack of sleep, making me more emotional or something.

"Then?" Andy says, of course.

Knowing it won't make sense, I say, "It's this damned stupid last name of ours. Hershberger. How many Hershbergers do you know?"

"Offhand? One."

"Exactly. Well, he was in class and this kid—I mean, college kid, you know—turned to him after roll call and asked him if he was related to that . . . that Hershberger bitch on TV who killed Kevin Cooper."

Hissss.

There must be an acid leak from the popcorn ceiling or something, because there's that burning sensation in my eyes

again. Noah gives me a sympathetic look; I hadn't told him
this particular part yet.

"Ouch," Andy says.

"Yeah. I thought, um . . ."

My throat constricts.

"You thought what?"

I can only speak if I keep my molars crushed tightly
together. Makes for an interesting speech impediment.

"I thought he'd defend me," I say through those teeth.
"Some asshole just called his little sister a bitch and he just
takes it? Backs down? What the . . . *God*!"

I suck my lips between my teeth, clamp down hard. For all
the things to be upset about, somehow reliving this scene the way
Jack shouted it at me that day hurts worst. *Just like Kevin,* I can't
stop myself from thinking. *Jack and Kevin both, two people who
don't have the guts to stand up for themselves. Or, say, their sisters.*

After a moment Andy says, "What's your favorite song?"

Noah and I both look at the phone.

"*What?*" I say.

"Favorite song."

"Are you, like, trying to change the subject for me?"

"Something like that."

"You're a *real gem*, Andrew."

He laughs, once, abruptly. "Thanks. Favorite song."

I sniff, unwilling to admit I appreciate the shift in topics.
"That's a completely unfair question. Song favorites change all
the time."

"True. Give me your favorite right now. Today's top song. How about you, Noah?"

"Today?" Noah says. "Uh . . . 'Kaze,' by Chatmonchy."

"Hmm. Not sure you spoke English there, but okay, moving on. Tori?"

"Ummm . . . okay, how about 'Respect and Fear' by Just This Once? I was listening to that this morning."

"You're asking me."

"Huh?"

"You said, 'How about,' as if there was a right answer. There's no right answer. I'm just curious."

"Oh. So what's yours?"

"Today?"

"No, yesterday." I said it as sarcastically as I could manage.

"Yesterday it was 'Can't Buy Me Love' by the Beatles."

"Okay, I was totally kidding about the yesterday thing."

"I know. Today I think it's 'I Got You Babe' by Sonny and Cher."

"Who?"

"Never mind. Look them up. Favorite food."

"Today?"

"Anytime."

"Well . . . honestly, my dad's garlic mashed potatoes."

Noah makes an orgasmic sound, which actually brings a quick smile to my face.

"He usually only makes them on Thanksgiving, but also on my birthday," I go on while Noah feigns being stoned by the mere mention of the dish. "I could eat it every day of my life, but I think the waiting makes it even better."

I don't mention he made them tonight and no one had any. My smile disappears.

"I gotta back Tor up on that one," Noah says. "I've had them. They are *really* good."

"What's he do with it?" Andy asks. "I mean, how are his different from every grandmother's on the planet?"

"I'm not entirely sure, but I think there's some kind of alcohol in it. Wine, maybe. I don't know. I don't *care*. I just want a bucket of it. Ah, God. Thanks, Andy. Now I'm craving it."

"Sorry."

I hear him yawn. So he's human after all. I let myself yawn in response. Noah only grins.

"Well," Andy says, "I want to say thank you for playing with me tonight."

"Playing?" I say. "So this was a joke, then?"

"No. Not a joke. Maybe I'll even get it right this time."

Probably because I'm so tired, it takes a couple of seconds for the meaning of his words to sink in. "Wait, *this* time? You mean you've tried to . . . do this before?"

Andy chuckles. "Still can't quite make yourself say 'suicide,' can you?"

I don't bother commenting on the accuracy of his observation.

"That's okay, I understand," Andy says. "Yeah. Once."

"Yeah, you once tried to?"

"Yes, ma'am."

I can't stop myself from asking, "How?"

"Tylenol. You know, it's amazing how easy it is to find ways to kill yourself. You ever think of that?"

As a matter of actual fact, I had, but wasn't for one second going to admit it to Andy.

"I suppose," I said. "So what happened?"

"It wasn't pretty. A friend of mine found me and took me to the hospital. They make you eat this charcoal stuff, and the next thing you know, it's coming out of every hole in your body, including a couple you didn't even know you had."

"That's disgusting."

"I think that was the idea. They treat you like shit, too. The nurses and doctors and stuff. No coddling. They don't want you coming back."

"But you *are* willing to go back." It slips out before I can stop to analyze what it might sound like.

"Hell, no. Why do you think I'm driving over a cliff? Get it done right."

God. Dammit. "So you are still thinking about it."

Andy takes a deep breath while Noah frowns down at the phone.

"You know something, Tori? It's been a real hoot and a holler talking to you tonight. It really has. You too, Noah old buddy."

Noah winces. "Um . . ."

"So I want to say thank you for that," Andy goes on before

Noah can say anything else. "But the fact is, a few hours ago now, I asked you for one reason. One reason not to drive off this cliff. And you never did give me one."

"Sure I did!"

"No, precious, you didn't."

Noah sits up and slides to the edge of the bed, like he's ready to run. I understand; I start to wake up too. Fast. "Oh. Okay. Well—"

"Nah, no. It's too late now. Because on the one hand, you've made me realize that, hey, I'm not the only one suffering out there. But on the other hand, Victoria Hershberger . . . you've killed any small piece of hope I might have had left. People are fucked up everywhere, and it's never going to stop, is it? So I want to say thank you for that, too. Thanks for confirming what brought me up here tonight. Now I know for sure I'm doing the right thing."

"Andy, don't!"

"Why. Not."

"Because!"

"That's not a reason."

"Because . . . maybe tomorrow will be better."

He chuckles again, but this time I can hear the exhaustion in it. "You don't think that, not really."

"But I *hope* so. I hope, Andy. That's all I got, man, come on." I turn to Noah and sock his shoulder, gesturing madly to the phone.

"Uh—yeah, yeah," Noah says, running a hand through his

hair. "You don't know what might happen tomorrow. Come on, hang in there."

Andy is silent for way too long, but since I don't hear anything else, I resist the urge to say his name, ask if he's all right.

"Okay," Andy says at last, and I surprise myself by exhaling a held breath. "Tell ya what, Tori. You've got till sunrise. Once that big orange bitch comes up, though, I'm going to light a cigarette, smoke it, and bid thee adieu."

I say, "Andy . . ."

Noah says, "Hey, man . . ."

"I'm on Route 57, outside Canyon City. It's west off the I-10."

"Andy, stop—"

"Did you catch that?"

"Yeah, fifty-seven, west off the ten, but look—"

"Whatever happens, Tori," Andy interrupts, "I really do thank you. No kidding. Okay? Thank you."

"*Where* on the fifty-seven? Tell me exactly where!"

"Just you, Tori," Andy says. "No offense, Noah, my good man, but if anyone else shows, I'm down and out. Got it?"

"I—I—I get it, yeah, but wait," Noah says.

"Bye, Victoria."

The line goes dead.

Tori Hershberger I'm kind of tired of school right now.

Like · Comment · Share · January 10

👍7 people like this.

Kevin Cooper me too, tori. sick of home too. pretty sick of fuckin everything.

👍You and 1 other person like this.

Marly DeSoto then stop coming! please!

👍4 people like this.

Dakota Lorey haha nice marly! yah stay home and spare us, team edward.

Albert Jiminez "dude looks like a lady" :)

👍5 people like this.

Lucas Mulcahy ha ya and he stinks teh place up hahaha

👍5 people like this.

Delmar Jackson bitch. Throw yourself down some stairs already

👍3 people like this.

Dakota Lorey delmar, who?

Steve Weide Maybe if we put out a petition to keep him off school property they'd have to not let him in!

👍4 people like this.

Delmar Jackson haha I ment cooper not you dakota :) your sexy

👍Dakota Lorey likes this.

Dakota Lorey aw, thanks.

👍Delmar Jackson likes this.

Marly DeSoto if kevin cooper asked me to prom you know wht Id say?

Kevin Cooper I WOULD NEVER ASK YOU TO PROM OR ANYWHERE! YOU SUCK AND PLEASE JUST STOP WTF DID I DO TO YOU????

Lucas Mulcahy youd say not even if you paid me to suck your dick after! shut the fuck up cooper you dum shit. Shut the fuck up faggit go die

Tori Hershberger It's okay, Super Duper Pooper Cooper. Your cock is still smaller than mine.

👍5 people like this.

Marly DeSoto hoo-ah, Hersh closing in on Lucas! nice job Tori. imagin life w/o Pooper. Ahhhhh ya!

👍You and 2 others like this.

Tori Hershberger Thanks, Marlycat. It's a gift.

Kevin Cooper you guys seriously just stop and leave me alone. theirs no reason to be like that. I really can't take this today okay so please quit!

Lucas Mulcahy shut the fuck up no one cares and no one likes you anyway so shut up

👍5 people like this.

Tori Hershberger Pooper Cooper, it's "there's." You missed an apostrophe and misspelled it. They covered it in fifth grade, as I recall. Consider returning?

👍You and 6 others like this.

FIFTEEN

I look at the tiny screen on my phone. Disconnected.

"No, no, no," I chant, and dial Andy's number. No answer. I hang up before it goes to voice mail. I try texting him instead:

> I'd have to take my brother's car and I'm not
> supposed to be driving.

I sit back down on the edge of my bed, waiting. A minute goes by, then another, then five. I am wide awake. Noah paces back and forth in front of me, his hand over his mouth.

"He didn't mean it," I say out loud. "There's no way. No way."

Noah stops. "We can't know that."

I send another text:

> Andy?

This time my phone vibrates with his response almost right away. Only two words.

Beautiful sunrise.

Oh, God. He's really going to do it.

Unless I can get there in time.

I shove the phone into my pocket and grab my shoes, pulling them on as fast as I can. "What time is sunrise?" I say, heading for the hallway.

Noah follows me, tapping furiously on his phone screen while I chew my lip practically off.

"Six forty-seven," he says.

We both look up at the cow clock.

Six ten.

I look into Noah's eyes. "Come with me."

"So you *are* going?"

"I have to!"

"Okay, but how?"

"Jack's car." I pick up his keys off the pegboard and hustle to the garage door. "Come with me, Noah, please!"

Noah licks his lips. "Tori, I . . . man, I would, I want to, but I think it's a bad idea. If we get there and it's both of us, you heard what he said. He asked for you."

"Noah!"

"Go," he says. "Look, I'll—I'll try to find you, drive past or something, but you have to go now. But, Tori, please. You've got to be careful, okay? You have half an hour. That's plenty of time. Don't drive stupid."

"Okay," I say. Then I reach up and hug Noah, tight. He hugs me back, even tighter.

"Thank you for being here tonight," I say.

"Anything for you," he says. "Now go. Just . . . go *safe*."

I nod and go out to the carport. When did it stop raining? An hour ago? Two? Doesn't matter. I stop when my hand hits Jack's driver's-side door.

"You can't be serious," I whisper to my ghostly reflection in the window. I'm not sure, but I think there are dark circles under my eyes. I remember I left the coffeemaker on, keeping the remnants warm, and that I forgot to put away the Coffee-mate. Mom'll be mad.

I start laughing. Hard. I have to jam my hand against my mouth to keep from screaming with laughter.

Mom'll be mad about the Coffee-mate while I'm out driving Jack's car up to the 57 to try to stop *yet another* guy from killing himself?

Really?

Shut up, I think. *You're losing it, Tori. Shut up, focus, get moving. Put yourself in the box. Eye on the ball. Now. Go!*

I get in the car, and wince when I turn the engine, wondering if anyone in the house can hear it. My heart pounds as I throw the gear into drive and move off down the street, trying to keep everything straight in my head: Stop at each sign, look left, look right, look left again, accelerate slowly, check the mirrors, don't brake too early or too late. . . .

I've got my license, but only by a few months. I'd just gotten it when everything with Kevin went down, and haven't really been on the road that much. I'm almost at the first major intersection by our neighborhood before realizing the headlights are off. Good God. I flip them on, scan the dashboard for indicators of any other important steps I might have missed, then turn onto the road that will take me to the 10, then the 57.

I keep both hands on the wheel and lean forward so far that my back begins to hurt. I *accelerate slowly* until I'm doing five miles over the speed limit, faster than I've ever driven before in my life.

I can see the road now without the lights on. Not well, but I can see it. The world is growing gray, the darkness slowly evaporating as I climb the mountain. Normally I'd enjoy the ride; the mountains are beautiful out here, dotted with proud saguaros and desert bushes. Normally I'd also be thrilled to be behind the wheel. Such a new experience, and signifying a transition to freedom unlike anything I'd known before. That is, of course, unless I was going to be in prison.

Can't think about that now, I tell myself. *Just keep your eyes open and look for a car pulled off to the side of the road.*

It only takes a few minutes to find the exit for the 57, which is obviously a rarely used mountain road. I take the exit, glad at least that it's too early for anyone else to really be clogging the 10 except for a few random big rigs.

I take my foot off the gas to rub my eyes, as if slowing from seventy to sixty-five will somehow be safer. Maybe it is. How should I know? I'm not even supposed to be here.

The switchbacks are making me dizzy, swerving left-right-left-right up the mountain, higher and higher, left-right, the world turning from grayscale to shades of blue and yellow and brown and—

There.

On my left, parked in the dirt, is a small white car. I don't know if it's a Sentra or not, because I'm not real big into cars, but it's got four doors and it just looks like something that would be called a "Sentra."

Sitting on the hood, knees doubled up, is a guy.

I hit the brakes and slow down.

He does not have black hair. He has light brown hair. And he's making eye contact, as if he knew exactly when I'd be rounding the corner.

I risk a quick U-turn on the highway. *Shit*, that was stupid. A big semi could've been rounding the corner and taken me out in a heartbeat.

But I live to do stupid things another day, and maneuver Jack's car until it's behind the Sentra.

I shut off the engine and take a deep breath.

Just as a cop car slows and pulls up behind me.

THE ARIZONA NEW TIMES

Horses vs. Humans
by Allison Summers
Why is shooting a horse's ass a felony but causing the death of a teenager isn't?

Kevin Cooper, 16, lived in the safe little enclave of Canyon City. He logged on to his Facebook account on the night of January 11, just like countless teens do every night. There, he left a message on a Friend's post—note the capital—and this Friend's Friends went on to leave comments of their own about him. None of them was kind. And at first it seemed like the sort of typical high school joshing everyone's familiar with.

But Kevin Cooper had had enough. On the website, he confronted this Friend and her Friends. Rather than respecting his wish to be left alone, the group dog-piled him with online insults and catcalls that would make a trucker blush. Time and again, Kevin tried to assert himself and get them to relent. But "relentless" is really the only correct term for what went on that terrible night.

A police report shows that within an hour of logging off, Kevin Cooper tied a long scarf around his neck, tied the other end to the balcony railing outside his room, and leaped.

This past summer, a 14-year-old Tucson boy was arrested for extreme cruelty to animals, a felony count that quite easily, and legally, booted him into the adult court system.

His crime: shooting BBs at two horses' asses. And we don't mean the state legislature.

For their part in urging Kevin Cooper to execute himself, seven Canyon High students face minor misdemeanor charges. At worst, they will receive ten to thirty hours of community service and up to a year of probation.

Not too high a price for virtually assassinating a gay kid. Yes, "virtually" has a double meaning here.

"Throw yourself down some stairs already," one student urges him in the Facebook comments.

"Imagin [sic] life w/o Pooper," says another post. "Ahhhhh ya!"

One particularly imaginative post reads, "Shut the fuck up faggit [sic] go die."

Harmless taunting? Hardly. When one considers the outcome—one more young human life lost to homophobic terrorizing despite viral Web campaigns like the It Gets Better Project—the concept of "harmless" doesn't seem appropriate.

continued

SIXTEEN

My life is over.

I sit in the car, shaking with lack of sleep, lack of food, relief at seeing Andy alive, and, well, terror that he might still do something stupid. Plus, there's this absolute paralysis now that a cop is climbing out of his patrol car and walking up to my car. My *brother's* car.

I don't know what to do. Are you supposed to stay in the car? Get out? Put your hands out the window?

"Morning," the cop calls.

My windows are still up, but I hear Andy call something back. He doesn't get off the hood of the Sentra.

The cop knocks on my window. I roll it down, praying my hands aren't really shaking as visibly as I know they are.

"What's the problem?" the cop says, peering into the car, checking out every nook and cranny.

"She's about an hour late is the problem!" Andy calls.

The cop looks over at him. He's still on the hood but now sits with his legs dangling over one side.

"What's that?" the cop says.

"I'm waiting for a tow, and my stupid little sister there was supposed to be here an hour ago to keep me company or give me a lift if the tow truck didn't show up," Andy says, shaking his head. He yells at me, "Thanks, Tori, *you're a real gem.*"

His lie is so effortless, so smooth, I nearly believe it myself for a second.

The cop cocks an eyebrow at him, then glances down at me.

"You having any trouble?" he asks me.

"No, sir," I say. "Just—yeah. Coming up to see him. Is all. Yeah."

"You worried about something?"

"Sorry, I've just never been pulled over before."

"I didn't pull you over. There something I should've pulled you over for?"

"No! No, sir. No."

"Got some bodies in the trunk?"

Ha-ha-ha-ha, you funny son of a . . .

"Nope, not me, no, sir."

The cop eyes me carefully, and I'm fairly certain my stomach liquefies and drains out of every open hole in my body. Hope I don't get any on his boots.

"All right, well, turn your hazards on," he tells me. "Same goes for you," he calls over to Andy.

"Oh, man," Andy says, giving him an embarrassed smile. "You're right, I'm sorry. Duh."

He hops down, reaches into the car, and the blinking hazard lights come on.

The cop nods. "Keep an eye out for traffic," he says, and walks back to his car.

I watch in the mirrors as he gets in. He sits there for approximately eighteen years, doing whatever it is cops do in their cars, before finally pulling back onto the 57 and driving down the hill, riding the brakes the whole time.

It's a very steep hill.

I sit back in the seat, close my eyes, and try not to puke out the window. Call it God, call it Flying Whatever Monster, but I swear someone was looking out for me.

It's about *time* I caught a break.

When I'm able to get my heart rate down to something less than two hundred, I open my eyes and stare at the car parked in front of me. The Sentra has no stickers, nothing to make it stand out. The license plate frame is from a local dealer.

Through the Sentra's rear window and on through the windshield, I can see that Andy has resumed his seat on the hood, just a little off center, kind of in front of the steering wheel.

I step out of the car and walk carefully over to the Sentra. The car is mostly dry, with little jewels of rain dotting the surface. Andy doesn't even turn to look at me. This nongesture strikes me as very cinematic. Staged. Still—it's effective.

"Just in time," he says.

I stand by the front fender, studying him. And, oddly, despite everything . . . he's kind of cute, I have to say. Not as cute as Lucas was, or maybe just cute differently, but cute.

Wait: As Lucas *was*? Past tense . . . ?

"Yeah?" I say to Andy.

"Well, maybe not *just*," he says, and supports his face in one cupped hand. "I'd say you had about, mmm, two more minutes before the sun—oops, wait! There it comes."

I turn to face east. The sun, which has been up solid now for a while, is only just beginning to crest a distant mountain. I've lived here my whole life, and I don't even know what the mountain is called. I really should start paying more attention to things.

"So when you said sunrise, you didn't mean from, like, the horizon," I say.

Andy shrugs. "I don't know. I hadn't decided."

And for some crazy-ass reason, I say, "So did I save your life or not?"

Andy finally turns his head to look at me. When he does, there's no study in it, no analysis. He looks at me like he's known me for years and isn't surprised by how I look, what I'm wearing . . . anything.

"Well," he says, "that's the big question, isn't it?"

Licking my lips, I point to the hood. "Can I join you?"

"I'd be offended if you didn't. I mean, after all we've been through together." He pats the hood.

I climb on. I sit with my knees up, like his, and wrap my arms around them, connecting them by grabbing my right wrist with my left hand.

"I thought you'd have long black hair," I say after a moment.

"Do I disappoint?"

"No," I say. "Not at all. What color are your eyes?"

He turns to me, raising what looks to me like a flirtatious eyebrow. "What do you think?"

"Blue," I say. Except they're not just blue; they're practically white. Like a husky's.

"Close enough," Andy says. "You handled the cop pretty well back there, by the way."

"Me?" I say, and almost manage to laugh. "You were freaking brilliant."

"Really."

I squint one eye at him. "Can I tell you something you may not know about yourself? You have a habit of phrasing things as statements that most people would phrase as questions."

"*Do* I."

This time I laugh. And Andy smiles.

"So. *Victoria*," Andy says. "Let's talk, shall we?"

My stomach grumbles. I ask him, "I don't suppose you have anything to eat by chance?"

"Backseat," he says. "Ice chest. Have at it."

"Thanks."

I slide off the hood and go to the rear passenger door,

which is unlocked. Inside is a basic blue ice chest. I notice a laptop resting on the passenger seat too, and wonder if he composed a suicide note on it. The thought chills me, and I focus on the ice chest. I open it up and find an assortment of food and drinks inside. Cokes, water bottles, apples, crackers, cookies in Ziploc plastic bags, all nestled between packages of that blue ice stuff.

It's a lot of food for someone not planning on being around much longer, but then again, I'd want to go out on a full stomach too. These are probably some of his favorites.

I grab a bag of oatmeal cookies and a bottle of water, and rejoin Andy on the hood. The cookies and water are unbelievably awesome. I'd been keeping on my softball diet, lots of protein and fruits, but what the hell. I didn't know hunger could make things taste so good. I haven't eaten since lunch yesterday.

"Okay," I say, after downing my first cookie practically whole. "Talk about what?"

"How about the trial?"

The cookie gets sticky in my throat. I have to wash it down with half a bottle of water.

"Um . . . it's just—"

"Oh, what, you're not supposed to talk about it?" Andy asks. "Please. You crossed that bridge quite a bit ago."

Good point.

"All right," I say. "What do you want to know?"

"What's the worst-case scenario? What could they do to you?"

"Well, the absolute worst possible thing is that they'll find me—us—no, wait, screw it, *me*. They'll find *me* guilty of all the charges."

Andy raises that eyebrow again. "Ah, suddenly your compatriots aren't quite as important."

I shrug. He might be right. Maybe I don't care so much about them anymore after all. Even Lucas. Broad shoulders and a good-looking face aren't much of a consolation if things go badly.

Andy says, "And if you're found guilty?"

"Then it would go to sentencing, and that could be up to ten years."

I wait for the inevitable drop in my stomach as I say the words, but it doesn't come. Maybe I'm getting used to the idea. Maybe I'm just too tired to care right now. I suddenly wonder if Noah has gone to sleep or not. Is he waiting up for me? Did he go home or wait at the house? Maybe he was able to find a car and he'll come cruising past like he said. That would be great.

"Ten years," Andy says, and shakes his head. "That's a long time."

"Yeah."

"So what's the *best*-case scenario, then?"

"Well, in a perfect world, I wouldn't be in this stupid mess in the first place. But since it's too late for that, I guess the best case is to be found not guilty on all charges. Or the case gets tossed out by the judge before the jury even gets to deliberate.

God, I really sound like I'm on *Law & Order* here."

"That's okay," Andy says. "I like *Law & Order*." He puts his chin on his arms and stares out over the valley. "That's a lot to have on your mind, huh?"

"I guess."

I shove another cookie into my mouth and chew it carefully. I'm not sure how much more I want to tell Andy about this. Mostly because it makes me feel a little sick. It makes me sick the way Jack—until tonight, anyway—wouldn't talk to me, or even look at me. How Mom isn't quite as affectionate as she usually is. How Dad hasn't smiled since he got the call from the school that day last month that the police had just picked me up.

Suddenly furious again, I spit out, "I didn't even talk to him. To Kevin. I mean, in person. At school. I barely even noticed if he posted something or not."

"Correct me if I'm wrong," Andy says, "but you barely noticed *him*."

For a second I feel betrayed, punched in the gut. That makes me mad.

"Hang on," I say. "That's a bunch of crap."

"What, am I wrong?"

"It's not—yes! No. Look, lots of people feel ignored, okay? I have. *You* have. It's not something unique, it's not something Kevin Cooper got to call all his own, all right? Lots of people feel alone and don't jump off a balcony with a scarf around their neck."

Andy says, "How many *want* to, I wonder?"

I ignore him and keep going with my point. "I'm just say-ing that it's high school, all right? Everyone gets depressed, everyone feels alone, this is not a new phenomenon. Maybe I felt that way too, until I met some new people."

"True, it's not a new phenomenon, but it's not usually fatal."

"Oh, *Jesus* . . . !"

"What about him?"

I shake my head. Come to think of it, what am I still doing here? Andy's out of his car; he's clearly not emotional. Isn't it safe to say this is one guy who won't be throwing himself off a cliff anytime soon?

"If there's some kind of karma or whatever, for whatever it is people think I did, I'm getting it, okay?" I say. "You want to talk about being alone? Swing by my house the past month, or the foreseeable future as far as I can tell. I'll show you what alone looks like."

"I never said he was alone," Andy says. "I said you didn't notice him. Not unless you were laughing at him, anyway."

"I *teased* him sometimes," I say. "As a friend. I'm not a *bully*."

"Well, what do you mean, whatever people *think* you did? Is what you did different from what the prosecutors are charging you with?"

"I didn't do anything! Haven't I been over this? I made a joke on a website—"

"More than one joke, wasn't it?"

"—*two or three* jokes on a social networking website and

a guy killed himself. And that is sad. And that is tragic. And I wish it hadn't happened. But *I didn't kill him.*"

Andy shrugs.

"I wrote a letter," I say, and even *I* can hear the whine in my voice. Why do I feel like I'm losing some kind of battle here?

"A letter," Andy says.

"To his mom? You know. *Apologizing?*"

I see Andy's jaw clenching and unclenching behind closed lips. "Well," he says, "that was . . . nice of you. What did it say?"

"I dunno," I say, and Andy snorts. "I mean, I said I was sorry, and it wasn't . . . I don't *know*, just that I was sorry."

"But she took you to court anyway."

I rub my eyes. "No. That had nothing to do with Mrs. Cooper. It had to do with this bitch Allison Summers, who's a reporter and got a bug up her ass. Wants to make a big media case, sell more papers, win a Pulitzer or something. . . . I dunno. Mr. Halpern tried to explain it, but I kind of glazed over."

"Who's Mr. Halpern?"

"My lawyer."

"He any good?"

"I guess we'll see. He'd better be, 'cause I'm not going to U of A anymore for it."

"But, strictly speaking, unless they find you guilty and put you away till you're twenty-six, you do get to go to college if you want," Andy says.

Twenty-six.

Twenty. Six.

That's a long time away. Twenty-six.

"And if they did put you in prison, even after you got out," Andy goes on, "or, if I'm not mistaken, probably even while you were in there, you could still finish school. That's something, right? That's more than . . . some people got right now. Maybe you should be more grateful."

I glance over at him again. Andy's face seems more relaxed than it did a minute ago. It's hard to keep up with this guy.

"So how are you?" I say pointedly, *beyond* ready to move on to a new topic.

"How am I, what?"

"How are you feeling? Are you still thinking about driving down this hill and over the edge, or what?"

Andy rears back a little, like he'd forgotten why he was parked at the top of a hill in the first place.

"Not really," he says, and unless I'm mistaken, he's actually smirking when he says it.

"So you're safe? I can get my brother's car back before he wakes up? I can finally get some sleep?"

The smirk falls off Andy's face, and I wonder if I've just completely blown it.

"Tori," he says, "you didn't have to come up here."

"No, Andy, I kind of did."

Andy slides off the hood and stands, putting his hands on the hood and leaning forward toward me.

"No, Victoria, you kind of didn't," he says. "Nobody forced you to come up here. I'm glad you did, I really am. But a lot of people wouldn't have. Especially not on the eve of, shall we say, so momentous a day as you're facing. Do you get that?"

Maybe I get it, but maybe also my eyes are so tired and dried out I feel like scratching them with my fingernails. And the oblique reference to my plea today sends tremors up my legs and down my arms.

"Well, anyway," Andy says. "Regardless, it was cool of you to come up here. But I understand needing to get home. It *has* been a long night."

"We should do it again sometime," I say, joking mostly out of exhaustion, and then it snaps into my brain how many different ways that sentence could be heard. One way is, *Hey, let's me and you get together sometime.*

Andy doesn't move. Only watches me.

"It's just that except for Noah, no one else is really talking to me," I say, for clarification. Andy is definitely not my type. "Not even the people I thought were my friends."

"Your co-conspirators?" Andy asks, but not in a mean way.

"No, the team. My girls. I thought we . . . I mean, that I could count on them, and . . . it would just be nice to be able to talk to someone or see someone who doesn't hate my guts."

I think I see something shift in Andy's eyes, but it's hard to tell with the rising sun lighting right into my face.

"Tell you what," he says. "Call me sometime. You'll get your answer."

Cryptic, but who cares. It's something.

"Thanks," I say, not even sure anymore if I mean it.

"Don't thank me yet."

Clearly enjoying that little send-off, Andy moves to the door, so I slide off the hood and walk around to that side as well, toward my car. Sorry, Jack's car.

"Are you going to be okay?" I say.

Andy turns back to face me. "Actually, yes," he says. "Thank you for asking. Seriously."

"No problem."

"No problem," Andy mutters back, so quiet I can barcly hear him. Not sure why he's repeating it. He starts to duck into the car, but I stop him again because there's just one tiny detail I need to know before heading home and putting this whole weird-ass night behind me.

"Andy."

"Hmm?"

"When you first called me tonight. Who were you trying to call?"

"I told you. It was random."

"You just punched in seven numbers and hoped someone would answer?"

"Sure."

"No offense . . . but that's bullshit."

Andy grins.

"Okay, maybe not random, exactly," he says. "More of a misdial."

"So who were you trying to call?"

Andy's grin blossoms into a smile. He opens the driver's

door, gets in, shuts the door behind him. Starts the engine. Rolls down the window.

"Suicide hotline," he says. "I must've hit eight instead of nine at the end."

"You mean my number, *my* cell phone, is one digit away from a suicide hotline number?"

"I know," Andy says. "Crazy, isn't it?"

He guns the motor.

"Take it easy, Vic," he says, and, after checking for traffic, pulls onto the 57 and drives on down the hill.

Ugh. Vic. Even under these bizarre circumstances, I hate being called Vic. Must be why Jack does it so much.

There isn't any traffic yet at this time of day, and I watch the little white car until it hits the first switchback. Waiting, I guess, to make sure he's really going to stay on the road and not, you know, *drive off it*.

I get into the car and start it up. Then, again maybe just because I'm that wiped out, I decide to call Andy back. Right now. Now that he's on the road, and safe, I'm going to call and tell him he can squarely go screw himself for dragging me through all this tonight.

I dial Andy's number with the last gasps of battery life on my phone. He doesn't answer, though. It's way too easy to imagine him checking the screen, seeing it's me, and laughing, tossing the phone onto the seat beside him.

I'm about to hang up when the voice mail kicks in.

And when it does, my stomach lurches sideways, wrapping

around my spine in something like terror. Like an icy hand gripped my intestines and spun them on a merry-go-round.

I listen to the entire outgoing voice mail message, which must last only five seconds at most, but which in my body feels like decades. I am old by the time it ends with a beep, older than a high school kid, older than my dad, older than sin.

I do not leave a message. I barely have the strength to tap the end-call button.

Andy lied.

About how much, I don't know. Maybe all of it, maybe some of it, but he lied. And did an exquisite job of it. Maybe Andy's not even his name.

I throw my phone into the seat beside me, and tear off down the highway as fast as I dare, trying to catch up with the fleeing Sentra. Andy can't be too far ahead of me; I could possibly catch up with him before he ever reaches an intersection to town.

I play no music, speak no words aloud or in my head. Just hear the voice mail message skipping over and over from beyond death.

It's not an accident, not a mistake, and not a misunderstanding. It's him.

"Hey, this is Kevin, leave me a message. Later!"

THE ARIZONA NEW TIMES

Horses vs. Humans

(continued from first op-ed page)

"Kevin wasn't very athletic," his mother, Cindy Cooper, reports, struggling to keep her tears in check. "Even back when I was in school, that was always important. The popular people were good at sports, and I wasn't. So I got teased. Everyone gets teased. I don't argue that. But to launch a campaign of relentless attacks on my son because he couldn't, what? Catch a ball? That's absurd and, I'm sorry, sinful."

A relentless campaign, she said. There's that word again.

The genius responsible for the "faggit" comment was not alone. Other commenters left similar remarks regarding Kevin's sexuality. The irony, if one dare call it that, is that there's no proof Kevin was, in fact, gay.

The question is: Does that matter? Should it? For certainly the people behind the comments—not identified here because of their ages—seemed to think he was homosexual and thus worthy of aggravated ridicule and demonization.

"This online bullying thing, it's out of control," Cooper says. "The things these kids say to each other, even things adults say. It's awful, awful stuff. Things you'd never say face-to-face. These kids who tormented Kevin, they're cowards. They're monsters hiding behind Wi-Fi, as if there aren't real people on the other end of the screen. Well, there are. Maybe if they'd thought of that, Kevin would be alive today."

What will Kevin Cooper's legacy be? That's in the hands of the courts now. But rest assured, we'll be watching.

So will every Kevin Cooper in the state.

~A. S.~

SEVENTEEN

Of course, of course, of course . . .

I will say this, think this, chant this until the world stops turning, if that's what it takes to make me fully accept the enormity of my stupidity.

So clear now. Not that it makes *sense*, because it doesn't, it makes no sense whatsoever, but of course there was something not right about this whole thing, this entire scenario, from Andy's phone call at midnight up till now.

And I bought it. Bought the entire story.

No, wait. I did not! Okay, there were a couple times during the conversation that I worried, that I wondered if he was really in danger. But from the very beginning, didn't I think it was a prank?

How much of Andy's story is true? How much of it could possibly *be* true?

And, most important . . . who the hell is he, and how'd he get Kevin's phone?

For one instant I wonder if I'm in some weird horror story, and that Andy is really Kevin, back from the dead, back to haunt me, back to take me to my own grave.

Except ghosts probably don't need ice chests full of food. No, a ghost would be easier. Less frightening.

The ice chest in the back of his Sentra, the laptop in the passenger seat. Like a . . . my God, like a *stakeout*. He had been up there since at least midnight, maybe earlier. That part was probably true; I'd heard the rain, and the Doppler-effect truck horn as it whipped past him.

And how could he have known my cell phone number ended with an eight? After everything that happened, he really still remembered the suicide hotline phone number? No. He knew my phone number, or had it written down. It was that simple.

But why?

And once again, for anyone just tuning in: *Who?* Who is Andy, and/or who put him up to this? A cop, a detective, some investigator or reporter, even a lawyer maybe . . .

Or—is it revenge?

The oatmeal cookies rumble in my stomach. Poison, maybe. How easy would it be to get away with that, under the circumstances?

I curve to the right and onto a downslope straightaway. I don't see the Sentra. How fast was he going?

No, no, no! I can't have lost him, there's no way, where could he poss—

Gas station.

I spot him standing beside the Sentra at a gas pump in a 7-Eleven parking lot. I stomp on the brakes—thank God it's early morning still and we're outside the main drag so no one rear-ends me. I feel badass for a second, like I'm on a cop show, as I twist the wheel to the right and onto a side street connecting to the gas station parking lot.

I pull into the gas station right behind him. Andy—if that's his name—doesn't even look up, but I can already see his smirk. He knows it's me.

I shut off the car and leap out, racing toward him.

"Who the fuck are you?"

"Why, hello, Victoria," he says, not taking his eyes off the ticking gallon meter. "Nice to see you again so soon."

"I should call the cops on you, you bastard."

"Oh? And accuse me of what?"

"I don't know! Who are you, dammit?"

The pump stops pumping, and Andy puts the handle back in its cradle. Still not looking at me, he begins screwing the gas cap back on.

"Who do you think I am?" he finally says.

"Stop it!" I scream. "Just tell me!"

Once he has the cap back on and the little gate shut, Andy finally turns to face me. His face is neutral.

"My name," he says, "is Andrew Christopher Stein. I'm

eighteen years old. I live in Flagstaff. And until tonight, you and I have never met. Does that help?"

Flagstaff . . . that's twenty miles north of here. And the name doesn't sound familiar at all, no more than the name "Andy" did seven hours ago.

"Why did you do this? You were never really going to kill yourself."

"Not tonight, no. But, Victoria, I have to tell you right now, about ninety percent or more of everything I did say tonight was the God's honest truth. I don't suppose you're inclined to believe that, and that's fine. But, well, there it is."

"How did you get Kevin's phone?"

Andy smirks again. "Ya know, I thought I heard the phone ring on the way down the mountain. Was that *you*, by any chance?"

Whatever he's doing, whatever he's up to, he's sure enjoying it. I fall back against the hood of my car. My shoulders drop, and I can tell my face droops like that of a five-year-old who doesn't get dessert.

"You left a message, I assume," Andy goes on. "Funny thing is, I don't know Kevin's password. I don't think his mom does either. The cops can probably get in there one way or another, I'm sure, but I can't. I doubt they'd bother, though. It's really not relevant to the case, or else they wouldn't have given it back to Cindy. That's Kevin's mom, by the way. But maybe you already knew that from court documents."

"I know who his mom is."

"Ah, right," Andy says. "From school, yeah? Or maybe you hung out at his house when you were little kids?"

"No! I did not go to his house, we didn't . . ."

I bite my lip. I've told him way too much tonight as it is.

"Who are you for real?" I say. "Please?"

The smirk disappears from Andy's face. He moves to lean against the trunk of the Sentra so we're facing each other.

"I saw the Facebook posts. But then, I guess, who hasn't? It's so funny to me that people think they can take down a page and it's gone from the Web forever. So lame. There's copies all over. I also saw your, uh . . . 'apology' letter. The one I'm sure someone forced you to write. Maybe your parents, or the principal, maybe even your lawyer, who knows. And yes, you did say you were sorry. But were you really? *Are* you? Are you really sorry, Victoria?"

My throat closes up. Spigots whirl behind my eyes and start to leak hot water.

No. I will not cry in front of him. I will not cry in front of this lying *asshole*. I don't even know why I'm suddenly wanting to cry in the first place.

Except—I do know.

"I'm sorry," I say. "I *am* sorry, and I've said it a thousand times."

"Sorry that you played an active role in killing Kevin, or sorry that you got caught?" Andy demands. "Sorry that Kevin will never see another sunrise like we just did, or sorry that this is putting a temporary snag in the rest of your life?"

"I didn't kill him!"

Andy looks like he wants to shout something back but holds it in. After a second, and to my shock, he goes, "I know."

I stare at him.

"I know that," Andy says. "You didn't tie the scarf around his neck, which, by the way, was a gift for his sixteenth birthday. And you didn't shove him over the balcony in the backyard."

Andy's voice now turns sharp enough to shred tires.

"No, Tori, all *you* did was add your two-cent little jokes, trying to look cool in front of a bunch of other people. You didn't know he had issues before this. Maybe he would have done it anyway. Maybe you weren't the straw that broke his back."

I nod. Yes, yes, see? This is exactly what I've been trying to tell people since it happened.

Andy narrows his eyes.

"But you didn't help him either. You watched. You just sat there safe on the other side of the screen and watched, and even threw gasoline on the fire. For what? So some senior would text you a smiley face or something? Maybe give you a nod in the hallway sometime?"

My face, my body, become wax, melting under his words.

His dead-center words, pointed and perfect as a sniper.

"Was it worth it, Tori?"

"No," I whisper. Because it wasn't. It *isn't*. They were so cool, and—you know. *Big.* Mature. Marly and Lucas and all them. Gearing up to run the school after the class ahead of them had finished up. I wanted that. I'd seen what happened to the Jacks of our school, and what a waste of four years it had been. I wanted something more for my time. That's all.

Andy doesn't seem to hear that I'd just agreed with him.

"At the end of the day," he says, "you don't think you did anything wrong. Or maybe you do, and you're just not grown up enough to own it. Which is it?"

I bring my palms up to my eyes and jam the heels into them. I don't feel like crying anymore. So that's something. But I don't feel real good, either. I twist my hands, burrowing them deeper and deeper into my eye sockets, hoping to rub away whatever it is that's making my flesh melt.

"How's that sittin'?" Andy asks.

"I'm . . . not sure." Which is honest enough.

"Well, lemme know when you figure it out."

"What issues?"

"Say what?"

"You said Kevin had 'issues,'" I say. "What kind? What was wrong?"

"Depression," Andy says. "He was on medication for it. One of those ones that says a possible side effect is suicidal thoughts. Ain't that just a riot? I'm sure your lawyer will figure that out, and it'll come out in the trial. It'll probably be enough to get you and your little buddies off scot-free." He shakes his head. "Whatever. It doesn't matter."

I nod, exhausted. Fair enough. I guess it doesn't.

"You still haven't told me who you are," I say. "Are you like a cop or something?"

Andy grins, sort of halfway. "Even if I was," he says, "nothing you've said could be used in the trial. There's no way. Go ahead and tell your lawyer whatever you want. Tell him everything, in fact. He'll probably be pretty pissed at you for telling me so much, but he'll also tell you it's no big deal. I can't do a damn thing with anything you've said."

Just to be sure, I say, "So you're *not* a cop."

"Wow, I really think you've missed the point of this little exercise. I should've known."

Since I believe him about not being a cop, my anger starts to swell again. "There was a point?"

"You haven't gotten it yet, have you."

Again with the statement-not-a-question. "I feel like shit, wasn't that it?" I say. "I feel horrible, okay?"

"Well, that's good. I'm glad. But that's not why I did this."

Andy steps over to me and, shockingly, puts one hand on my shoulder. I'm so amazed that he'd make physical contact that I practically do a backflip over Jack's Civic. Once my instincts settle down, Andy peers at me, making sure I don't avoid his eyes.

Andy says, almost kindly, "A few hours ago, a guy you'd never met said he needed help. You couldn't be sure he was even telling the truth. But you stayed up all night, *stole a car* . . . went halfway across a city . . . *and* drove up a mountain in the dark, not knowing what you'd find when you got there. Basically, you did everything in your power to help. You took risks, you didn't worry about the consequences, or what people might think about you. You just saw that something had to be done, and you did it. So whatever else you may be, I think there's hope for you, even if you were doing it to cover your own ass. At least it was something."

Andy drops his hand. I strangely miss the warmth of it. He takes one step back, still giving me the piercing-eye treatment, and shakes his head a little bit.

"I just wonder," he says, "where that girl was when Kevin needed her."

I lick my lips. I don't know what hurts more: the truth, or the shame of it.

Something else worries me too, even though it really probably shouldn't.

"Do you hate me?" I ask.

"I'm not your biggest fan, no," Andy says, moving backward till he hits his car again. "But I don't hate you. Anymore. I did. All of you. All of you on that goddam Web page. But that doesn't solve anything. I'm getting over it."

"Why me?" I ask. "Why'd you pick me? There's six other people in trouble."

"Because you're special."

"Special how?"

"You'll see. Eventually. And by the way—it was 'Fallout.'"

"What?" I say. He's changing topics so fast. No wonder I

bought into his BS. The guy knows how to manipulate people. Or me, at any rate.

"And," he goes on, "believe it or not, salami and pepperoni sandwiches. In a pita, with balsamic vinaigrette. It's like a canker sore waiting to happen."

"What are you *talking* about?"

"'Fallout' is the name of Kevin's favorite song. 'Fallout.' By a band called Black Cymbal. Like a drum cymbal, not like symbolic. Although I guess a cymbal could be symbolic, I never really thought about it. And his favorite food was salami and pepperoni sandwiches."

"Why are you telling me that?"

Andy looks upward as if at the sky, except the gas pumps are under a tall canopy. The gesture strikes me as melodramatic.

"Because I want you to think for a second—no, a full minute at least, I think he deserves that—I want you to think for a minute what it would be like to never hear your favorite song again. Ever. Never taste your dad's garlic mashed potatoes again. Ever. Why? Well, because you're dead."

I swallow hard. Melodrama or not . . . it stings.

"Because that's what being dead means," Andy says. "It's the zenith of 'never.' Never again, never this, never that. You don't come back from never. You can't enjoy never. You just sit there, not existing, not listening to your favorite songs or eating your favorite foods. Never."

He pauses.

"You just sit. And rot. And smell."

"You are a morbid asshole."

I say this because he is frankly scaring the Jesus out of me. But then, Jesus got to come back.

Andy isn't impressed. He shrugs. "I've had a lot of time to think about it. Especially after the Tylenol incident. Which, by the way, was very much a true story. Maybe if *you'd* thought about it, we wouldn't be having this conversation."

For a second I feel like maybe I'm going to throw up, but I don't. Still, my jaw gets that awful rubbery feeling and my knees tingle.

"What do you want from me?" I say, like my tongue is swollen and thick. "What did you want me to do, huh?"

"I wanted you to drive across the mountains in the middle of the night to make a difference."

Totally confused, I shake my head and say, "I did that, I did do that, I'm standing right here!"

Andy lifts his palms. "Then how hard would it have been to write a Facebook response saying, 'Hey, leave the guy alone'? Instead, you chose to perpetrate a hate crime."

And that, as they say, *does it.* I practically snap in half.

"How can it be a hate crime if he wasn't gay?" I demand. "That's ridiculous, it's a ridiculous charge!"

"It was a hate crime because you hated him," Andy says.

"I didn't *hate* Kevin."

"No?"

"No!"

Andy shrugs. "Okay, fine," he says. "So you didn't hate him. You were just indifferent. Which is actually a lot worse."

"Oh my God, who the hell do you think you are, Jesus Christ himself?"

"Oh no. No. Not at all. Jesus forgave people. I'm under no such obligation."

"I'm innocent!" I scream, so loud and hard that I bend at the waist and squeeze my eyes shut.

It doesn't seem to impress Andy, who merely blinks back at me.

"No," he says, "you're *not guilty*. There's a whole big gulf between innocent and not guilty. You won't be in court today and plead innocent, you'll plead not guilty. Two very, very different things, if you ask me. So sure. Maybe you're not guilty. Innocent?" He gives one shake of his head to the side.

Which reminds me, with sudden and awful clarity, that I'll be going before a judge just a few hours from now to give my plea. Oh, God.

Well, time enough for that later. Right now, I need the truth from Andy.

"Who *are* you?" I croak. It'll be a while before my vocal cords are back to normal.

"It doesn't matter now."

I keep pushing. "In relation to him. To Kevin. Who are you to Kevin?"

Andy smiles, but it makes his eyes wince.

"I'd think less about who I am," Andy says, "and more about who I was."

"Well, that's nice and stupidly cryptic."

"Oh, I'm sorry, did you think I owed you more? Suffer." He opens the car door. "You'll figure it out," he adds. "One more thing. I don't have a girlfriend."

"Of course not," I spit out. "That's part of the ten percent that was a lie, right? Great."

Andy, for the first time since I've known him—since midnight—laughs out loud.

"*Wow* are you dense," he says.

With that, Andy puts a foot into the car, ready to climb in.

"You should get home," he says gently. "You look wiped out. Sorry about that. Except, you know, not really."

"Whatever," I say.

"Take care, Tori," Andy says. His face is set in a neutral mask. He climbs into the Sentra and drives carefully out of the gas station, leaving me alone.

I wait until I can't see the Sentra anymore before climbing into Jack's car and heading for home. I flip the sun visor down, only barely considering what Dad's likely to do to me when he finds out I took Jack's car, never mind what Jack might do. But then, Jack hates me anyway, so no loss there.

Mostly I don't care. I mean, seriously, what could Dad possibly do to make my life worse right now? Take away my phone? He's welcome to it. Not let me out of the house? Sure— oh, except for court dates, I guess. . . .

I take my time getting home, and even stop for a coffee and bagel, figuring why not. The bagel is gone and the coffee halfway to being so when I pull up to the house.

Jack is sitting on our front porch. Uh-oh.

"Okay," I say out loud as I park my brother's car. "Here we go."

EIGHTEEN

I close the car door carefully, gently, knowing Jack is watching my every move. Then I start up the carport and hang a left onto the front porch. Jack's kicking back in one of the garden chairs Mom keeps out here, and he's watching me watch him.

I walk up the three steps to the porch and keep moving toward the front door.

"Have a seat," Jack says. His voice is barely within the area code of "pleasant."

I hesitate, then sit beside him in another chair. Jack smiles but shows no teeth. He's not amused, not having fun. I guess the smile is designed to make me feel better somehow, only it doesn't. No one in my family has smiled at me in a month.

"Can I have my keys?" he asks me.

I hand them over. "So, what, are you talking to me now?"

"Yes," Jack says, bouncing in his chair as he nods.

His answer catches me off guard. "What? Why now?"

"Because there's a lot to talk about."

"Like what?" I ask, taking a drink from my still-hot coffee.

"Andy Stein."

I choke on the drink. "Andy?" I sputter, feeling liquid drip down my chin and scald me. "How do you know about him?"

"You were on the phone all night with him."

"How did you know that was his *name*?"

"Because I'm the one who gave him your number."

A mourning dove whistles in the corner of our small yard. Low, *high*, low . . . low . . . low.

"Can you—say that again?"

But even as I ask the question, I know it's true.

Of course it is. It makes sense now, at least in terms of how Andy got in touch with me. And he called me Vic, something only Jack does. I should've realized it before.

"Forget it," I say. "I heard you the first time. Jack . . . what the *hell*, man?"

"You saw what I went through in high school," Jack says, gesturing to the worst of his acne scars. "But that didn't stop you from picking on another kid. I don't get that, Vic, I really don't."

Jack's right about how people treated him, and I know it. It was pretty awful. Sitting here on the porch with him, I remember days when he'd refuse to go to school because of a horrific breakout, and the things people would say to him that I only knew about because he'd repeat them to Mom and Dad, screaming, even crying. It was hell for him for a while.

That's what Kevin felt like?

"I don't know what Mr. Halpern told you," Jack says, snapping me back to the present. "But the truth is, holding someone really, legally responsible for someone else's suicide is super hard to pull off."

He pauses and sits back in his chair again, looking out at the street. It's too early for traffic, and our neighborhood is peaceful.

"You're going to get away with this," Jack says.

I don't like the way he phrases it but don't bother to argue.

Maybe he's right to put it that way.

"They might convict you of some lesser deal," Jack goes on. "Like the harassment, maybe, or something like that. But let's call this what it is. You're a sixteen-year-old white female with no prior record who made a bad joke on the Internet to a kid already diagnosed with depression. That's it. That's how it'll come out in the end. You'll get some community service, maybe probation or something, and that'll be that. Don't worry, kid. You're not going to prison."

I wish that idea made me feel better.

The front door opens then, and Noah squeezes through. He shuts the door so quietly, I assume Mom and Dad must still be asleep.

"Hey," Noah says.

I stare at him, trying to melt him with my brain waves. I feel like . . . like I've been cheated on, somehow.

"You were in on this?" I say.

"Well . . . yeah." Noah moves to sort of sit-lean against the porch railing, on Jack's side, so my brother is between us.

"So tonight, when I called you after dinner, you knew this was going to happen?"

"Yeah," Noah says. "I tried to end it. Remember, I told you to turn off your phone and just go to sleep? I had second thoughts. But then . . ."

Noah shrugs.

"How could you do this to me? After everything I've been through?"

Noah blows out a breath and looks at Jack. Jack leans forward toward me.

"We were trying to help you," my brother says.

"Help me," I say, and almost—actually, nowhere near almost—laugh at him, because now I sound like Andy, phrasing questions as statements. "Don't you mean punish me? That's what this is, isn't it? In case we're all let go, or, or . . . acquitted or whatever?"

"Punish you?" Noah says. "Have you even heard yourself these past few months? I hardly recognize you, Tori. This isn't you, this isn't the person—"

"You could've just *said* that instead of faking all this!"

"I did! I did *just say it*, all the time! I said it tonight on the phone, and you still didn't hear me." Noah makes a face like he wants to spit on the floor. He stands up straight, taking himself off the railing. "What is it you see in those people, anyway?"

"What do you mean, *those* people?"

"You know who," Noah says. "The same ones who were charged? The ones who wrote all that stuff on Kevin's car . . ."

"I tried to fix that," I say. "I went to his house myself to clean it up and the car wasn't there."

"Did you, uh, *knock*?" Jack asks.

I glare at him, but it's perfunctory. "The point is I tried. And, besides, I didn't know they were going to do that. I said I was sorry."

"Okay, that's great, but why hang around them *at all* after that?" Noah insists.

"Because . . . everyone looks up to them."

"*Not* everyone," Noah says. "Trust me on that."

"Look," I say, "friends . . . change, okay? It's normal, it happens, *that's* what happened." I go to take a drink from my coffee, change my mind, sit back in my chair. It's hard to keep from pouting, which is not something I do regularly anyway.

"Friends change," I say again.

"Maybe," Jack says, "but it doesn't usually get them killed."

"So that's it, then. You all—all of you think I *killed* Kevin."

"No. It's not that," Jack starts, but Noah jumps in.

"It's that this wouldn't have happened a year ago," he says. "You wouldn't have let it. And I—well, Jesus, Tori, I miss you, okay? And I promise you, I *swear* to you, those assholes you're trying to hang with do not."

The mourning dove coos again from one of the trees in our yard. Low-*high* . . . low . . . low . . . low . . .

In the relative silence, as I feel the warmth from my coffee cup slip away and fade into the morning, I know they're right. A year ago I just wanted to keep playing ball. A year ago I was happy that Noah and Kevin still talked to me.

What I told Andy, about feeling alone, that wasn't a lie. High school was big, and freaky, and scary, and my older brother who was a senior at the time could barely manage it. How was I supposed to fare? So I kept my head down and played ball, and suddenly the varsity girls were paying attention. Then their baseball-playing boyfriends were paying attention. And the next thing I knew . . .

But who do I have now?

Jack stands up. "Look, Vic," he says. "I don't care who your friends are, who you hang out with. Whatever. And I don't blame you for anything. You're my sister, and I love you. Okay? But Noah is right. This whole mess? It's not you. I know you better. *He* knows you better. I think Andy said everything I wanted you to hear, and I knew you wouldn't hear it if I said it. So, I'm gonna leave it at that."

My brother puts his hand on the doorknob but hesitates.

"And I'm sorry for cutting you out," he says. "I was mad. And embarrassed. But I'm here. I'll be there in court today too. If you'll still let me."

He goes inside, closing the door quietly behind him.

I try a sip of coffee. It's gone cold. I sip again anyway, and turn to Noah.

"How'd you know I'd call Kevin's cell this morning?" I ask him, and my voice is starting to croak.

Noah almost laughs. "Oh, we didn't. That wasn't supposed to happen. We were going to sit you down tonight. Like an, uh . . . what is it. Intervention."

I shove my elbows deep into my gut and lean forward over them, desperate to get the truth from him. "Why couldn't we just talk about this, Noah? Why did you have to go through all this stuff tonight?"

"Like I said, I tried," Noah says. "I swear. I wanted to get your attention, but with Lucas and them . . . I couldn't compete. You have no idea how much I've wanted to—"

He shuts himself down, fast.

"God, I'm afraid to ask. Wanted to what?"

Even though he's standing and I'm sitting, he somehow manages to peek *upward* at me.

"Nothing," he says. "Don't worry about it. Just wishful thinking."

I set my coffee down on the table between my chair and Jack's, and move to stand beside Noah. I put my hands on the railing surrounding the porch, looking out at our street. Our hands, our pinky fingers, are almost touching. There's no more than a whisper of warmth between them.

"Was all that stuff Andy said about his girlfriend even true?"

Noah blinks. "Girlfriend?"

"Andy's girlfriend, Kayla. She ran her car off the road? But at the gas station, he said he didn't have a girlfriend, so I figured he made the story up entirely. . . ."

"Tori," Noah goes, "no offense, but you know how some people are what they call 'sharp as a tack'? Sometimes you're about as sharp as a Post-it."

"What?"

"No, he didn't have a girlfriend. Um, *ever*. Do the math, Hershy."

Tori, you stupid, stupid bitch, is the first thought to race through what's left of my mind. How did I miss it? Maybe because Andy was a real good actor, okay maybe, but come on.

"So Kevin really was . . ."

"Uh, yeah."

"With Andy."

"Uh, yeah."

"Meeting at the comic shop, the Superman movie . . ."

"Everything except the car going off the road, yes."

I swallow. Whatever's in my mouth, it tastes bitter. The implications of this are pretty freaking awful on a number of levels.

"What about Rachel?"

"Yeah," Noah says, scratching his head. "She kinda wondered but didn't ask questions. And I mean, Kevin was a nice guy. Who'd blame her? Then when he met Andy, Rachel found out and ended it."

"Who else knows?"

"Me, you now, and Jack. Rachel, but she'd never bring it up. As far as I know, that's it. He died without telling his mom, even. Nobody knows for sure, but the way Andy tells it, she might not've been entirely supportive if he'd come out to her."

That makes me stop for a second. I can understand not wanting to be out in high school, even at some of the more accepting places around the country. And Canyon sure isn't one of them. And I know Mom and Dad are upset about this mess I'm in, but I can't imagine not being able to tell them something. That has to suck.

Of course, this train of thought brings me back around to my favorite subject: me. My needs, my fears, my worst-case scenario.

"If Andy tells anyone that Kevin really was gay," I say to Noah, "if he can prove they were together—"

"He's not telling anyone, Tori."

I try swallowing again, only this time I can't make the muscles work.

"How come?"

"Because that was never the point. The point was to . . . get you back. I mean, get *you* back. The old you. The you *I* liked."

The old me. The old me feels like a really long time ago. I'm not sure I'd recognize her. For one insane moment I want to say, "You mean *like me*, like me, or just *like* me?" as if we were still in junior high.

Instead I say, "Liked, as in, past tense?"

"No. No, sorry. I didn't mean it like that. Promise."

I accept that. Noah's not a liar. Well, except for the whole fraudulent phone call thing.

"So what was in it for him?" I ask Noah. "I never *met* Andy. Why'd he go to all this trouble?"

Noah takes a long, deep breath through his nose, like he's not sure he should answer. Then he says, "He was talking shit about you. And I told him he was wrong. We had a pretty long fight—er, argument, I mean. But then afterward we sort of came up with this idea. Brought Jack in, 'cause I knew he was pissed too. I wanted to prove you weren't awful, and Andy wanted . . . I dunno, to see if I was right."

"Wait, how'd you even meet him?" I ask, scanning my memory for some moment where I'd crossed paths with Andy. The fact that he was angry isn't exactly a surprise. "Where was he talking shit?"

"At the funeral."

My eyes bulge. "You went to Kevin's funeral? Why?"

"Because I knew him, Tori. From junior high. I mean, we didn't hang out a lot or anything, but we were cool."

"Did *you* ever defend him?"

I expect this brilliant riposte to freeze him up, but Noah only sighs.

"No," he says. "I didn't, not really. I never saw the posts— you know, those last posts—until it was too late. But there were times before that I could've said something. Don't think that hasn't bugged the crap out of me ever since."

I wait for him to add more, but he doesn't.

"If I change my plea today, maybe it'll, you know, *say* something," I say. I suddenly really need Noah to be *okay* with me.

"Say something? You mean like, making a point?"

"I guess. Maybe it would help."

"It might. Or it might just be a sideshow. You should probably do whatever's best for you. But I see what you're getting at. It's a nice thought."

I almost say thanks, but that seems stupid, trite, and overall dumb. So I don't say anything, and neither does Noah. Not for a long time. We just look out over my yard. More birds are singing now. The storm clouds from last night are virtually gone.

Finally Noah turns his head. He holds my gaze for a couple of seconds, during which I'm pretty sure some kind of signal gets transmitted between us, like the minuscule head shakes a pitcher gives a catcher: *Pitch it here, not there. No. Pitch it this way, not that. Yes.*

Noah starts to lean toward me—but stops, pulls back, looks down. Shakes his head, ever so slightly. Licks his lips. Looks up at me again.

"Listen," he says. "When this is all over, the trial and everything, when you have time to think again, maybe we can—"

I have nothing to lose, and I'm pretty sure I read the signal right. So before he can finish, I lean up and kiss him quickly. Just once.

"Or, you know, now would be okay too," Noah says, his eyes wide.

"Okay, so that wasn't just me," I say.

"No. Huh-uh. No."

"Okay. Good." I pause. "Sorry."

"Don't be," Noah says, and slowly begins to smile. "Yeah, definitely do not be sorry."

Except, I am. Just not about Noah.

We both face out again. Whatever just happened, it's a relief to think about something nice for a change.

"What about Lucas?" Noah asks me a moment later.

I shake my head. "I'm over it."

"Well, no offense, but thank God."

"Yeah," I say.

When another minute goes by without either of us saying anything, Noah abruptly says, "So, I'm gonna go." He takes a step toward the stairs. "If you want to call me after the thing today . . . I'll be around."

"Cool. I probably will. But I might also be asleep for like eighteen hours."

"Right. See ya later, Tori-chan."

He takes the stairs slowly, heads down the carport, and hangs a left, headed toward his house, hands in his pockets. Unexpectedly, I feel more than hear Andy's words at the gas station vibrating in my head. *You're special. You'll see. Eventually.* And I get it. I wait till Noah's a few yards down the sidewalk.

"Noah."

He stops, looks back.

"Thanks."

Noah smiles a bit. "Sure. *Sayonara.*"

He says it with what I believe is perfectly accented Japanese: *Sigh-oh-nada.* I say it back to him, making it as American as I can: *Say-oh-nair-ah.* It makes Noah laugh, and then he's gone.

I go inside. Mom is sitting at the breakfast bar with the newspaper spread out in front of her. A fresh pot of coffee sits on the counter. She must've been up for a while, then, and gone to get a new bag of coffee, and saw Jack's car gone, and *me* gone. . . .

I guess she wasn't asleep all this time after all.

Mom doesn't even bother raising her voice as she says, "Whatever it was, I certainly hope it was worth it."

"Yeah," I say. "It was."

I can tell my voice sounds weird. Different. Because Mom looks up then, frowning.

"Whatever you want to do to me, that's cool," I say. "I'm sorry I took the car. But, actually, not really. I'd do it again under the circumstances."

I'm almost surprised to hear myself say it, honestly.

Mom lets the corner of the paper she's been holding flutter to the counter. "What circumstances?" she says. "What have you been up to all night? And why was Jack still up? He won't tell me anything."

"Maybe later, Mom," I say. "Sorry."

She nods, clearly not convinced. "All right," she says. "You should get some sleep. We need to be out of here by noon."

"That's the plan. Mom?"

"Mmm?"

"Do you think I'm guilty?"

Mom sits up straight on the stool. "Tori . . ."

"It's just, you never actually said."

Mom clears her throat a little. "I . . . ," she says slowly, "expected better from you."

Right. I suppose I did too.

"Okay," I say. "G'night."

"Good morning, you mean."

"G'morning."

Mom gives me a small smile and goes back to her paper. I can hear Dad snoring down the hall.

Sounds good to me.

I go into my room, shut the door, and plug my phone into its charger. Sunlight bleeds through my blinds, casting everything in orange. I pull off my shirt and sit on my bed to yank off my shoes. Holy crap, I've never been so exhausted in my life.

My life.

Still got it. Whatever happens when the trial begins, I'll still have that.

I almost fall asleep sitting up, peeling my socks off. They're drenched in stale sweat.

My bed feels so warm, so ready to let me pass out and forget this night ever happened. Except . . .

I probably shouldn't do it, but if Andy's right about the

password, then what the hell. It'll just be between us.

Leaving my phone plugged in, I dial Andy's—Kevin's— number. Sure enough, neither Andy nor anyone else actually answers. I assume Andy's still got the phone, and that he's probably asleep already himself. Or still driving back to Flagstaff. How many times did he make that drive to be with Kevin? Could he make it out here every week so they could hang out?

"Hey, this is Kevin, leave me a message. Later!"

"Hi, it's . . ."

I stop. I don't want to identify myself. It occurs to me that my number will obviously be on the phone's memory again, but I still don't want to say my name.

". . . It doesn't matter," I say. "I just, I wanted to say . . . I wanted to tell you that I'm sorry, Kevin. It's too late now, I know that, and . . . I wish I could go back. So I'm sorry. I really am. No matter what else, I just need you to know that somehow. If that's even possible. I don't know. But I'm sorry."

I stop again, trying to figure out how on earth to end this call. How to summarize everything that's happened.

I choose the simplest.

"Bye, Kevin."